AHEAD OF THE

(Westcountry Sp'

By the same author

Sharks in British Seas (Shark Cornwall Publishing)
Sharks off Devon & Cornwall (Tor Mark Press)
Pirates of Devon & Cornwall (Shark Cornwall Publishing)
The Poachers Moon (Struik Nature, Penguin Random House)
Giant Steps (Struik Nature, Penguin Random House)
Execution Sites in Devon & Cornwall (Shark Cornwall Publishing)
Shark Attack Britain (Shark Cornwall Publishing)
Nicole (Struik Nature, Penguin Random House)
Westcountry Witches, Wizards & Warlocks (Shark Cornwall
Publishing)
Cuddle Me, Kill Me (Struik Nature, Penguin Random House)
The UK Great White Shark Enigma (Shark Cornwall Publishing)
Orca (Struik Nature, Penguin Random House)
Pangolins, Scales of Injustice (Struik Nature, Penguin Random House)
66 True Kalahari Stories
Westcountry Outlaws, Highwaymen & Rogues (Shark Cornwall
Publishing)
Top Secret in the Westcountry Until Now!? (Shark Cornwall
Publishing)
50 Westcountry Heroes, Villains & Famous Characters (Shark
Cornwall Publishing)
Kalahari Gold (Heritage Publishing)

AHEAD OF THE GAME

Westcountry Spy Attack

Richard Peirce

(This novel is fiction)

SHARK CORNWALL PUBLISHING

AHEAD OF THE GAME
© Richard Peirce 2025
Address: 20, Dean Clarke House
Southernhay
Exeter, Devon
United Kingdom EX1 1AP
Published in the UK by Shark Cornwall Publishing

Web address for orders: www.outstandingmd.co.uk Tel +44 (0) 1208 73171 **or**
rpaconsult@peirceshark.com
UK cell no: +44(0) 7836 606325

Editor: Nellie Alberts
Design & layout: Stella Stofberg
Cover design: Beth Paisley
Icons: Frey Wazza
Photographs from Shutterstock

Typeset in Palatino Linotype 11 on 16
First edition, first print 2025
ISBN 978-0-9558694-0-2
Printed by Short Run Press Limited

DEDICATION

To the men and women working in all the branches of the
United Kingdom's intelligence services

THANKS and ACKNOWLEDGMENTS

My thanks to the following for their help, advice, and support.

Nellie Alberts	Hugh Monro
Karl Bennett	Jeremy O' Shanohun
Robert Bluett	Beth Paisley
Benn Cunningham	Michelle Panter
Matt Devenish	Frankie Panter
Alison Gordon	Chris Pringle
Angus Gordon	Sharon Roberts
Falcon Hotel, Bude	Stella Stofberg
Nick May	Paul Vincent
	Sophie Vincent (Rock Marine)

and last but not least, my wife Jacqui

Contents Page

List of Characters
(Alphabetical)

Ahmed (Syrian Angler)
Akram (Syrian Diver)
Alexei (Assassin)
Angus and Alison Gordon
Axl Symonds
Captain England-Kerr
Captain Pandelis
Christian Single
Christine (MI6)
Cole Benson
Colonel Igor Petrov (GRU)
Corporal Tod Pollard
Daniel (MI6)
Daoud (Syrian Angler)
Dimitry Volkov (aka Igor Petrov)
Dylan (Bartender)
Fiona Edworthy
Frankie Pinter
George (M16)
Gerald Richmond
Handy Andy
Henry (MI6)

Hugh and Clare McLeod
Jill English
June Symonds
Madeleine Richmond
Magd Dossari
Michelle Bolt
Mohammed (Syrian Diver)
Pete Vicko
Reuben Symonds
Richard Matson
Roger Watney (MI6 Deceased)
Ron Berry
Rosalind (Ros MI6)
Stefanie Tanner
Suleiman (Syrian Angler)
Svetlana Petrov
Tim Oxley (Ox)
Tom Edworthy
Vincent Headon
William (MI6)
Yevgeny (Assassin)

PART ONE

The Forces of Good and Evil

1

*B*ude 2024

Gerald Richmond read the anonymous text message which simply said, "Roger Watney has died, please call the sender, this is an open line."

The text had been deliberately worded to convey three messages: It identified the sender, requested a return call and advised discretion when making the call.

The message brought back memories of a dinner in Beirut years before where he had been recruited to work for the Secret Intelligence Service (SIS), known to most people as MI6.

Roger Watney had been the senior member of a three-person M16 team working under diplomatic cover in the British Embassy in Beirut. Gerald's father, Colonel John Richmond, was one of many Britons working in sensitive Middle East positions who regularly provided intelligence to MI6. Colonel Richmond was living in Beirut but had been on leave in the UK when he died two years previously. A few months after his father died Gerald and and his wife Madeleine, whose name was often shortened to Maddie, moved to Lebanon's capital Beirut.

Gerald and Maddie were nomads. Both were the offspring of British army officers and both had spent much of their early lives moving on whenever their fathers got new army postings. They had lived in several African and Middle Eastern countries and were as much at home in the bush or the desert as in their native United Kingdom. They had married young, and with their children grown up they pursued lives of adventure and exploration.

They made a good-looking couple and anyone watching carefully would realise they had a close relationship. They both looked younger than their years, but their eyes and conversation spoke of decades of experience. At 5 ft 10 in with midbrown coloured hair and a slight build Gerald didn't stand out in a crowd but his demeanour was that of a man who not only could take care of himself, but who could also be dangerous if opposed. His restless eyes were constantly scanning the area around him. He displayed an economy of movement but could act with lightning speed when necessary.

Brunette, bubbly, with a throaty laugh; unflappable and stoic in a crisis, Maddie was a long-suffering wife who often wished they would settle down. However, she relished the action, fun and adventure of being married to Gerald, a man known for being quietly contemplative but with the sharpest reactions and the ability to act explosively.

The couple were keen wildlife conservationists who now split their time between homes in South Africa and Cornwall. Gerald was the author of several books and made documentary films, all trying to advance the protection of wildlife and the natural world. He and Maddie firmly believed that humanity had lost its way, and would eventually lose the battle to bend Mother Nature to its will. The couple devoted a considerable amount of their time and money trying to increase awareness of environmental and conservation issues.

Gerald had been sitting, having a cup of coffee and watching the sea from the balcony of his house in North Cornwall when his phone had buzzed. He frowned as he reread the message.

Roger Watney dead!

Six months after settling in Beirut, all those years ago, Gerald had received a call out of the blue from Roger Watney at the British Embassy. Watney said he was an old friend of Gerald's father and invited him to dinner in a downtown Lebanese restaurant near Beirut's port. Roger had to have been aware of Gerald's devotion to his father because he used this as a lever to recruit him as an agent for MI6. Roger explained to Gerald that his father had had excellent access to many leading figures in the Middle East, and thus was able to provide valuable intelligence. According to Roger, Gerald's father had informed him that his son was planning to move to Lebanon, and had recommended him for work with the Service.

MI6 is tasked with gathering intelligence and conducting operations outside Britain's borders; MI5, its sister organisation, operates within the UK, concentrating on counter terrorism operations, watching suspicious foreign nationals living in the UK, managing surveillance of potential enemies of the state, and liaising with MI6, the police and other agencies to counter internal threats to Britain and its citizens. It is not uncommon for the work of the various agencies to overlap and competition between them is frequent.

The first assignment Roger offered Gerald involved him and Maddie living in an apartment paid for by MI6, sharing a floor with the Bulgarian Embassy in a building in Beirut. This was during the Cold War, and Bulgaria was firmly in the orbit of the Union of Soviet Socialist Republics (USSR), known today more simply as Russia. All over the world the USSR and the West were involved in a continual intelligence competition, and being a hardline ally of the USSR meant Bulgaria was on the other side and of great intelligence interest to Britain and her Western Allies.

Holes would be quietly and carefully drilled into walls, listening devices and tape recorders would be installed. Every few days the tapes would be collected by Roger or an MI6 colleague. This had been the beginning of Gerald undertaking regular work for the intelligence agency. The work had ended only two years before the arrival of the enigmatic text.

As soon as Gerald read the message he knew from whom it was. A smile played on his lips as he speculated why the Service was getting in touch again. He was an old-school spy and had felt more comfortable in the past world where intelligence was gathered by humans rather than the hi-tech gadget-led information gathering which was now dominant. He missed the excitement, adrenalin, potential danger and challenge which were part of secret intelligence gathering. MI6 was operating against governments and individuals which might threaten Britain, and so almost by definition, was often working outside the law when operating in foreign countries.

Clandestine operations overseas routinely meant working in ways which avoided detection. This behaviour generally known as tradecraft, dictated the way agents lived and worked.

Gerald had spent so many years avoiding detection – identifying when he was being followed or watched, doing brush-past contacts, servicing dead letter drops, and following subjects of interest without being detected himself – that these habits often resurfaced even though he was no longer an active agent.

His work for MI6 and time spent living and working in several of the world's trouble spots had led to his developing a range of defence mechanisms. In restaurants or other public places he always tried to sit with his back to a wall so no surprises could come from behind and he could watch a room and see who was coming and going. If possible, he would sit against a wall with an exit door nearby, and when walking in the street he always checked the roofs of buildings for watchers or snipers. When driving he would quickly spot a tail, and when walking, anyone following too closely behind him, made him suspicious and uncomfortable.

Gerald made the call which was brief. A woman called Rosalind, who suggested she be called Ros, answered immediately. Gerald thought the odds were high that neither Ros nor Rosalind was her real name. Ros requested a meeting as soon as possible, and three days later Gerald made the journey from North Cornwall to London. He met Ros in Rules Restaurant where he was offered a new job.

When he received the text a few days ago, he wondered why MI6 was getting in touch with him again. He wasn't a modern electronic spy. In his time, face to face action, playing different roles, and being able to forge relationships, were what was important.

As he listened to Ros's muted conversation over lunch it became apparent that a previous relationship and Gerald's personal people skills put him in a unique position to help MI6 deal with a very serious threat to Britain. The action involved in the operation would take place within the UK, probably mostly in the south-west of England. Technically this should be MI5 rather than MI6 territory. However, Ros had liaised with her opposite number in MI5 and made the case that MI6 should lead because she claimed that her agent would only work with her agency. When she explained this, Gerald smiled inwardly as he realised he had been used in the forever ongoing turf wars between "Five" and "Six".

After lunch he caught a late afternoon train back to Exeter from Paddington and as he stared out of the window he realised he hadn't felt so alive for quite a while. He missed being involved in covert operations, and this time he would be working against an old and familiar enemy. After the train left Reading a series of events began which would show that not only had Gerald not lost his edge, but also reminded him that adrenalin and risk were important parts of his life.

The other occupants of Gerald's First Class carriage were two couples, an elderly woman, two young women and three men, all of whom were travelling separately. As is normal for British travellers no one spoke to anyone except those who were travelling together. The light was starting to fade as Gerald watched the overbuilt countryside flash by outside his window.

Three youths had got on the train at Reading and were making their way through the carriage looking for the catering coach so they could buy more alcohol to add to the large quantities they had already consumed. They entered Gerald's carriage and walked past him. One of the young women passengers was wearing a short skirt and was world's away listening to music on her ear pod. She had not realised that her skirt had ridden up her thighs and her pair of yellow panties was now exposed.

"Fuckin 'ell! Look at that, you can almost see 'er fanny."

Everyone in the carriage looked up to see the three men laughing and leering at the girl who blushed bright red and pulled her skirt down, wishing she had worn something else. The girl was sitting alone at a table for four and the three youths flopped into the spare seats around her.

Gerald watched and wondered whether the lads were just half-drunk harmless noisy yobs, or whether a potentially dangerous incident would evolve.

The girl was enveloped in a cloud of alcohol fumes and felt very threatened as the lad sitting next to her moved closer, making sure their thighs were touching. The youth opposite stared and was wearing a smile which conveyed menace and threat.

"I've never done it on a train before, 'ave you, Tel?"

"No, John, I 'aven't," and he turned to the girl, "'Ave you, darling, I mean, 'ave you ever 'ad a shag on a train?"

She was now trapped and terrified. She pleaded, "Please let

me out, I want to move."

"Nah, darlin', that's alright, you just stay 'ere and look after us."

She desperately hoped that either the train conductor would arrive or the other passengers would help her. A young man sitting two rows away got up and left the carriage and was immediately followed by one of the two couples.

The youth called Tel watched them and remarked, "Must 'ave been something we said, lads." They all laughed and he continued, "We'll soon be on our own, darlin'; then we can 'ave some fun. What's your name then, eh?"

She looked pleadingly across at the couple sitting nearest to her and answered, "You are not getting my name or anything else. Now let me go." She half got up and tried to get past John who pushed her roughly back into her seat.

Oh dear, thought Gerald, who continued watching while opening his shoulder bag and taking out an eight inch long black cylinder which looked like a torch.

"Well, Tel, I think I might 'ave a little shave," said John as he drew a lock knife from inside his jacket, opened the blade and placed it on the table. Almost as if acting on a pre-agreed signal the remaining occupants of the carriage got up and left.

"Now we are all alone," said John as he undid his belt buckle and unzipped his fly. He turned to the girl. "Why don't you come and sit on my lap, darlin'?"

"We ain't alone," observed Tel, "there is that old geezer down there at the end." He nodded at Gerald who sat calmly watching events unfold.

"He ain't nuffing." John then called down the carriage to Gerald. "You ain't nuffing, are you mate? See, I told you, Tel."

John picked up his knife and pointed the blade at the girl. "Now then, darlin', knickers off and on my lap, there's a good girl."

The girl was sobbing as he half turned and reached between her legs to her panties.

Three things then happened all at once: The girl looked past John and her mouth dropped open in shock. A hand was holding John's knife at Tel's throat, and John twitched spasmodically as a blue light danced on his face, electricity crackled before he passed out.

Gerald held his laser type stun gun in one hand and John's knife in the other. Tel had gone white and the third youth suddenly felt sick with fear and alcohol. Gerald looked at the girl, "Climb over him and come to me."

She grabbed her rucksack, clambered over John who had started shivering and groaning, and stood behind Gerald. He zapped John again with the stun gun and moved the point of the knife to just below Tel's ear.

Tel's eyes followed the knife as it moved; he tried to sink back in his seat.

Gerald jerked the knife under Tel's ear and blood flowed immediately from a small cut. "John was going to have a little shave, Tel, would you like a little shave, too?" asked Gerald.

Tel was sure he was about to have his throat cut, and the warm wet sensation between his legs indicated that his bladder thought the same thing.

Gerald turned to the girl behind him, "Go back a few rows and sit down. Nothing will happen now; you are safe."

The train was now slowing down and Gerald spoke to Tel and the third youth. "Your friend will start coming round anytime now. The train is stopping. Pick him up, take him to the end of the carriage, and when the train stops, get off. If I ever see you again I won't borrow a knife or use a stun gun, I will shoot you." Gerald's dramatic threat sounded hollow even as he said it, but the boys were too drunk and frightened to see it as a bluff and said, "Yeah, yeah," while nodding vigorously.

19

They grabbed John under his armpits and dragged him to the end of the carriage.

Gerald sat down next to the girl who was still wide eyed and crying quietly.

"My God, my God, thank you so much. Have you got a gun as well?"

"No," answered Gerald, and as he did so the door slid open and the conductor appeared, followed by another member of the train staff.

"We heard there were some drunks in here threatening a girl," said the conductor.

The train had now stopped in a station, and rather than answer Gerald nodded at the window through which the two youths could be seen half dragging the semi-conscious John along the platform. "No real problem, they were just rather loud and I think, quite drunk. I guess this is their stop."

The conductor turned to the girl and asked, "Are you alright, Miss, is everything okay?"

"Thanks to this man, yes, he told them to leave me alone."

Well, that's one way of putting it, thought Gerald as he smiled innocently at the railway officials.

Maddie was waiting for Gerald at St David's Station. A brief hug and a kiss hello and she got straight to the point.

"Well, what did they want? Are you, are we working for them again?"

"Yes, we are, and this time we will be working from home. The Russians are coming to us."

"Hmmm, sounds interesting. You must tell me all about it on the way home. Apart from meeting our friend, was it a good trip, anything interesting happen?" She held his arm as they walked to their Range Rover.

"No, not really, some noisy drunks got on the train at Reading but I had a word with them and they got off at the next stop."

Maddie shot a glance at her husband. "Had a word with them and they got off? Alright, I won't ask, not now, anyway."

They drove out of Exeter, heading north-west home to Bude in Cornwall. Although a confirmed nomad North Cornwall was one of the places which Gerald thought of as home. He recalled a saying, "To be truly happy you have to live where the wind knows your name."

As always when heading to North Cornwall he felt the wind knew his name.

2

The GRU is Russia's foreign military intelligence agency which was created by Joseph Stalin in 1942. Over time there have been name changes and today its name is the Main Intelligence Directorate, but most people still refer to this agency by the three letters that were its label for decades. Much better known during the Cold War era was Russia's foreign intelligence and domestic security agency, the KGB. The GRU did not have the KGB's notoriety, but during the Cold War was responsible for many of Russia's most notable intelligence successes, including infiltrating the British nuclear weapons programme and recruiting up to seventy people in United States scientific and government institutions.

Following the end of the Cold War the FSB became the main successor to the KGB. Nowadays it deals with counter-intelligence, internal state security, and intelligence gathering in some countries, primarily former USSR satellites. The Main Intelligence Directorate (GRU) reports to the Minister of Defence and the Chief of the General Staff, while the other agencies, including the FSB, report directly to the president. However, in reality the Main Intelligence Directorate (GRU) today reports directly to President Putin, like the rest of the intelligence and security apparatus.

The Foreign Intelligence Service (SVR) succeeded the First Chief Directorate of the KGB, and also reports to the president. Its headquarters are in the Yasenevo district of Moscow. The operation which Russia intended to launch against the UK, and which MI6 had been tipped off about had, unusually, superceded interagency rivalry and had been jointly agreed by the FSB, SVR and the Main Intelligence Directorate (GRU). The plan had been taken to the president who approved it, but instructed that mercenaries be used, and Russian involvement disguised.

In 2005 Igor Petrov was a colonel in the GRU based at the Russian Trade Delegation in Highgate in London. At that time Gerald had been given the assignment of cultivating a relationship with Colonel Igor Petrov in the hope that he could be turned and recruited to work for MI6. Gerald had done very well and had developed a genuine friendship with Petrov who was a keen sea fisherman. Gerald had an encyclopedic knowledge of sharks and considerable experience of catching sharks off Cornwall to tag them for scientific research. At his first meeting with Petrov he was posing as a businessman who was interested in buying Russian weapons for an undisclosed client state. They chatted for long after the hour allotted for their meeting, with each man gently probing the other for both personal and professional information. During conversation Petrov had mentioned his interest in sea angling; this gave Gerald the opportunity to talk about his work with sharks and explain how he caught them on rod and line to tag for research.

After the meeting was over Igor Petrov ran extensive checks on Gerald. He was particularly interested on a personal level when Google and other research tools confirmed his work with sharks. Igor had never caught a shark, and the idea of a battle between him and a large marine predator was appealing. It appeared that his new friend might be able to arrange the opportunity which only increased his desire to get to know Gerald better.

Igor Petrov was born in 1951 in St Petersburg when the city was called Leningrad. His father was a middle-ranking member of the Communist Party, and it had been him that had encouraged Igor to join the army in which his uncle was a colonel in the artillery. He made good progress in the army, and later transferred to the GRU after developing a close friendship with a GRU officer when, as a senior lieutenant, he served in Kaliningrad. He enjoyed the intrigue of the intelligence world and the power of being an officer in the GRU. Igor was never a committed communist in terms of believing in the ideology, but he was a Russian patriot who thrived on serving his country. He had married aged 25 and had two sons. By the time Igor was in London posing as a trade representative at the mission in Highgate both of his sons had grown up. The elder of the two was working in the aerospace industry as a technician, and his younger son was at university in St Petersburg. One reason that Igor and his wife were happy to be in London was that various allowances paid due to his serving overseas were helping put their younger son through university.

Together both MI5 and MI6 routinely watched and kept track of foreign intelligence officers working under diplomatic cover at embassies in London. Those watching Igor judged that he was enjoying life in Britain, and might have leanings towards the West. Gerald had been given the assignment of getting close to Igor and trying to turn him into a friend. It was Gerald's job to get to know him well enough to judge whether he would be likely to respond positively to an approach by MI6. Compared to their Western counterparts Russian officers were often short of money, and those who weren't committed ideological communists could often be turned and recruited to spy for the West for money. Once Gerald had befriended Igor, earned his trust, and felt that a recruitment approach might succeed he would then arrange social occasions at which Igor would meet some of his friends. One of these friends would be the MI6 officer who would eventually try to recruit the Russian. Gerald hated handing over his targets to an MI6 recruiter because most of the time he believed that having become genuinely close to a target he would have the best chance of carrying out a successful recruitment. On more than one occasion in the past when recruitment approaches had failed Gerald had been sure that had he made the approach he would have succeeded. Although Gerald had often been proved right MI6 policy in this respect remained rigid, he understood this and knew it was partly for his own protection.

Gerald's cover story to Igor was that he had high level contacts in the Arab Gulf States who could influence the placing of multimillion dollar civil and military government contracts. The cover stood up to examination because both Gerald and his late father did genuinely have top-level contacts in the area. MI6 were kept informed by the Commercial Sections and Military Attachés of British embassies regarding the civil and military contracts that were planned in the Gulf. The information was passed to Gerald who visited the Russian Trade Delegation in Highgate every couple of weeks, and dangled the upcoming projects in front of Igor, claiming that his friends had inside tracks, which would win the contracts for those who paid generous commissions.

After their first meeting Igor had reported Gerald's approach to the GRU which had done thorough background checks into Gerald and his story. That Gerald's story had checked out well was due in no small measure to much of it being true. At many of their meetings Igor would steer the conversation to sea angling and to shark fishing off Cornwall. This was a gift for

Gerald because Igor was unwittingly setting himself up for an invitation to go shark fishing, and there would be an MI6 officer among Gerald's guests that day.

As if he were playing a fish Gerald slowly reeled Igor in, and when he asked him if he would like to go shark fishing from Bude in North Cornwall, Igor's response was enthusiastic. To cement the invitation Gerald suggested a weekend away, and said that his wife Maddie would be delighted to entertain Igor's wife while the men were at sea. Igor seemed keen but had to get approval from both Svetlana his wife and his GRU senior officer.

After each meeting in Igor's office Gerald gave a detailed debrief to the two MI6 officers who were his handlers. When Gerald told them of the possible visit to Cornwall by Igor and Svetlana Petrov, his colleagues were doubtful of the merit of involving Maddie and Svetlana, and thought that Igor's acceptance was unlikely. Gerald had a bet with his MI6 friends that not only would Igor accept the invitation for both him and his wife, but he would do so quickly.

Gerald won the bet. Three days later Igor called accepting the invitation, asking Gerald to recommend a hotel in Bude, requesting advice on appropriate clothing for a day at sea and asking for Maddie's number for Svetlana. MI6 was delighted to learn that Igor had accepted but remained unconvinced that involving the two wives was a good idea. Gerald's response was firm, he said he knew Igor, knew what he was doing and was confident that the wives' dimension would help firmly hook Igor in readiness for the MI6 recruitment approach.

To an outside observer the weekend would have looked like a casual fun event involving two couples and some friends. In fact, everything that happened had been planned in meticulous detail. Igor and Gerald went to sea on the Saturday on a small sea-angling charter boat skippered by a friend of Gerald's. Also on board were two of Gerald's friends, one was an unwitting local called Hugh and the other an MI6 officer called Daniel.

Their first fishing mark was nine miles offshore where they started a chum trail to attract Blue Sharks. While the men were steaming out to sea Maddie was driving Svetlana to Truro where they would have lunch and spend the day shopping. Daniel had given Maddie £1,000 in cash to buy lunch and also pay for items that Svetlana showed interest in.

If Svetlana accepted presents from Maddie it would help hook the Petrovs. When Igor discovered that Svetlana had accepted gifts from Maddie he would not be pleased because he would immediately recognise that this might have compromised him. However, he would have no reason to suspect that Gerald and Maddie were anything other than what they appeared. MI6 had recognised that there was a slight risk that Igor might become suspicious if Svetlana was given gifts, or the weekend went over the top in any other way. Gerald, however, was confident in his sixth sense, and insisted that if, at any time, he felt something was striking a wrong note with the Petrovs he would change the script and carry on as he felt appropriate.

At the first fishing mark Gerald caught a five foot female Blue Shark. He tried to give his rod to Igor so that he could play and boat the shark, but Igor had insisted that it was Gerald's rod which had come to life when the shark went for the bait, so it was right for Gerald to keep the fish. The shark was brought to the side of the boat, unhooked and released.

Igor produced a bottle of vodka from his rucksack and

insisted that everyone drank to Gerald's shark. An hour later Igor's rod came to life, at first with a couple of clicks on the reel, then the line screamed off as a newly-hooked shark made its bid for freedom.

"That's not a bluey," noted the skipper, as he checked that Igor had his belt on properly and was ready to fight his fish.

"No, a porbeagle, I reckon," agreed Gerald.

"Porbeagle shark, that is good," offered Igor who was flushed with excitement. He had let his shark run, then applied the brake on his reel, stopped the shark and began the slow process of reeling the big fish back to the boat.

Forty-five minues later Igor got his vodka bottle out again. After a lively battle he had landed a female porbeagle which, before they released her, Gerald estimated weighed 300 lbs. Igor was thrilled, he hugged his angling companions and the bottle of vodka was passed around continually. The others didn't notice that while Gerald and Daniel appeared to be drinking enthusiastically, the swigs they were taking were very small compared to the other three.

They drifted for another hour and continually refreshed the chum trail but there were no more hits on the baited lines. The others didn't realise that as soon as Igor had caught his shark it was job done for Gerald and Daniel, and although nothing was said they would have been happy to head for shore without trying for any more catches.

While steaming back the satellite dishes on the cliffs at RAF Cleave Camp to the north of Bude were plainly visible. Gerald and Daniel half expected Igor to ask what they were. When he didn't they both concluded that it was because not only was he fully aware that the dishes were part of the UK's GCHQ intelligence-gathering capability, but he also didn't want to appear interested.

Gerald had a slight smile to himself because Igor's lack

of interest was a giveaway. He had approached Bude from the sea with anglers on board dozens of times, and someone would always ask what the huge satellite dishes were for. The fact that Igor had ignored them sent a clear message.

Maddie and Svetlana had got on well and had a fun day in Truro. Apparently, as they later related at dinner, one of the highlights had been spotting a man dressed as a woman who had his hair dyed half pink and half green. It was obvious that Svetlana did not have a lot of money to spend, and Maddie bought her an item of jewellery, a dress and a pink jumper which she told Svetlana would go well with her hair if she decided to dye it pink!

She told her new Russian friend she had recently won £5,000 on Premium Bonds and wanted to treat her and anyway, Igor was having fun, so why shouldn't she? This approach did the trick and Svetlana relaxed and gratefully accepted all these gifts.

The day was a complete success and that evening Gerald, Maddie, Daniel and the Petrovs all had dinner together at the Falcon Hotel where Igor and Svetlana were staying. The high spirited evening stalled for a few seconds when Igor asked where all the spies lived in Bude.

No one knew what he was talking about but Gerald bought time by instantly replying with, "Do you mean the British spies, the CIA or the KGB?"

Igor thought Gerald's reply was hilarious and explained that he had heard that the British government had a satellite monitoring and listening station near Bude.

Touché, thought Gerald, who said that there was a large installation of satellite dishes on the cliffs near Bude which Igor must have noticed on their way in and out, to and from their fishing ground. Igor said he had noticed them and had wondered what they were and had meant to ask but had forgotten.

The conversation moved on and Igor and Gerald cemented their friendship. Daniel and Igor got on well enough for Daniel to invite Igor to lunch in London in the near future. This was a crucial part of the process of trying to recruit Igor because it would mark the start of Gerald phasing himself out and handing him over to Daniel.

Gerald, Maddie and Daniel left and the Petrovs went up to their room.

The weather forecast for the next day was fine and dry and Gerald had proposed they all go for a morning walk along the beach because it would be low tide, and then have lunch together before the Petrovs drove back to London.

Daniel was staying with Gerald and after they got home Maddie went up to bed, leaving the men to debrief each other on the day's events. They agreed that everything had gone as well as could be hoped for, and spent a few minutes trying to decide why Igor had popped up with his question about spies.

Gerald's view was that Igor was an experienced trained intelligence officer and thought he had deliberately asked the question to judge the reaction. Maddie had been talking to Svetlana and had carried on as if she hadn't heard, Svetlana had looked sharply at her husband, Daniel had laughed and Gerald had responded with his crack about the CIA and KGB.

Daniel agreed that Igor's remark probably had been a test, was confident their reactions would have given nothing away and would have allayed any suspicions Igor might have had.

After the successful weekend and following weeks of Gerald's hard and painstaking work the scene had been set for the attempt to recruit Igor.

However, it would all come to nothing because three weeks later, two days before Gerald and Daniel were to have lunch with Igor in London, Russia expelled three British diplomats from the embassy in Moscow on the basis that they were MI6 spies. Two of them were.

The expulsion would almost certainly be followed by a tit for tat reaction from Britain. Daniel was told that, despite his protests, it was almost sure that Igor would be one of those expelled.

Gerald rang Igor and said he would have to delay their lunch by a week because he had been called away on an urgent business trip. Five days later the British government sent a list to the Russian foreign ministry with four names on it, Igor was one of them. They had all been given seven days to leave Britain.

3

North Cornwall, 2024

On the drive home from Exeter to Bude, following his trip to London, Gerald gave Maddie a full rundown on his lunch at Rules with Ros. Many years earlier when Roger Watney had first recruited Gerald, Maddie had been fully vetted by MI6 and given a security clearance under the Offical Secrets Act. She had often been a part of some of the operations in which Gerald had been involved, and he felt fully justified and comfortable discussing issues with her which were classified secret.

Ros had got quickly to the point and told Gerald that MI6 needed him back for a special, unique assignment. She explained that Gerald's old friend, Igor Petrov, had retired from the GRU some years earlier and was now working both on his own and with a private intelligence group which at one time had been closely allied to Yevgeny Prigozhin's Wagner mercenary group, and which was often used by the Kremlin to carry out operations which the Russian government wanted to be deniable if necessary.

One of the few positive aspects of the war in Ukraine was that both before the war and subsequently both British and American intelligence agencies had well-placed agents right at the top of the Kremlin hierarchy and close to President Putin. This had enabled the West to be able to accurately interpret all Putin's preparations leading up to his invasion of Ukraine. Since the war started the flow of high quality intelligence had alerted MI6 to a plot against Britain's communications and electronic intelligence-gathering abilities by destroying the major government communications headquarters (GCHQ) installation at Cleave Camp near Bude in Cornwall. At the same time the transatlantic undersea cable owned by Google would also be blown up. The cable runs under Crooklets Beach and out to sea only four miles south of the GCHQ installation and carries a large portion of the UK's internet communications to and from the United States and Canada. The aims of the attacks would be to seriously degrade British capabilities, embarrass the British government and demonstrate to British citizens how vulnerable their country really was.

The KGB's successors, the FSB and the SVR, together with the Main Intelligence Directorate (GRU) had jointly developed the plan which had been given Kremlin approval with the proviso that it be carried out by independent contractors. If the operation went wrong for any reason the Kremlin would then be able to deny it had been an official Russian government action. The denial would not be believed in the West, but just having deniability was seen as necessary.

The MI6 sources had identified Colonel Igor Petrov as having been given command of the operation. His second-in-command would be an ex-special forces rogue Syrian called Magd Dossari. After leaving the Syrian army, Dossari had become a mercenary and an unoffical arms dealer selling mainly Russian weapons to terrorist groups and any countries or individuals who could further Russian interest. Magd Dossari would work with two teams each of three ex-Syrian special forces soldiers.

One team would attack the GCHQ installation from the sea with drones or missiles, and the other would blow up the undersea communications cable. Ros further explained that, probably due to his having been expelled from Britain, Petrov would be travelling under the false name of Dimitry Volkov. As he listened to his briefing Gerald realised that the MI6 Moscow

The GCHQ satellite dishes are on the clifftop near Morwenstow north of Bude. The dishes dominate many aspects of the land and seascape around Bude almost like eyes looking out for Britain's security

source was a priceless asset.

The MI6 plan envisaged keeping a close watch on Petrov, as soon as he arrived in Britain. MI6 would guide Gerald and a small team which would stay close to Petrov and Dossari and his men without actually becoming visible. Gerald's team would gather all the physical evidence they could as the Russians prepared for their attacks. The Russians would have to rent cars, charter a boat, maybe photograph and film their targets and take delivery of the equipment they would use to attack the GCHQ installation. Gerald's team would be the feet on the ground while MI6 techies would bug and eavesdrop on the Russians at every opportunity.

"We are ahead of the game on this one due to the intel which has given us advance warning; it should continue to keep us ahead of the game as we counter their operation. We want you and your team to dog their every move, and then when we have gathered enough evidence and judge it to be the right moment, probably as they are getting ready to attack, you will approach Petrov.

"We know that he dislikes the UK and could be hoping for an opportunity to get back at us because we expelled him. We have studied everything we could find which would help us analyse your relationship with him. We believe he genuinely liked you, and the irony is that we think he may have been working towards trying to recruit you, while you were doing the same to him.

"You will present him with all the evidence that we have known about his operation ever since he arrived in the UK and show him it is now well and truly blown. Initially he will be angry and frightened and probably resentful towards you once he discovers you are MI6 and were playing him all those years ago. However, ultimately he has to believe what he is being told, and we think he will believe you.

"Neither Igor nor any of his team will be in the UK with any sort of diplomatic cover and when we go public Moscow will certainly deny any knowledge or involvement. You will convince him that due to having no diplomatic cover we could put him on full public trial as a mercenary terrorist; he would spend the rest of his life in jail and never see his family again.

"Alternatively he could work for us. You would then give him two options, either he downloads to MI6 everything he knows past and present, and publicly identifies the Kremlin as being behind the operation. We put him on trial, he gets a new identity and disappears. Or we hang on to his guys and put them on trial to embarrass Moscow, but let him escape back to Moscow where he works for us. If he goes for it and opts not to return to Russia we would get his wife out before going public with anything.

"If we get lucky and he says yes to you and goes for option two, then we achieve the double whammy of turning the game against Moscow and getting a new well-placed source. If he says no we have all the evidence to convict them all and make Moscow look rather silly."

She continued, "The Russians always deny everything. The Novichok attack on Sergei Skripal and his daughter, the downing of the Malaysian Flight 370 and other events have been investigated and were clearly Russian operations but were always denied. This time if we have Petrov on record admitting it was a Russian operation, we may well be able to use that to make others in the team talk if we promise lighter sentences. Confessions from Petrov and his whole team would be a very powerful tool. Whichever way the detail of the end game works out we will have a very good chance of irrefutably proving Russian guilt and showing it to the world. Because we have an inside source we can keep ahead of the game all the time. It is a gift and we mustn't screw it up. The Russians will be aware this operation will be an attack on a NATO country which, worst case scenario, could put them at war with NATO; so they will certainly take steps to cover their tracks, which will make it all the more fun exposing them.

"In terms of the current intensity of geopolitics our political masters will be very happy if we pull it off. It will be a major coup for the Service; the Chief would buy us several large gins because it will certainly boost his chance of avoiding any budget cuts if the Chancellor starts wielding a money-saving axe. All to play for, Gerald."

Ros had stopped talking and Gerald held her gaze but said nothing for almost a minute. She had assumed Gerald would immediately agree to the proposition, but with every second that ticked by she became less sure.

"It could work, maybe it will work. OK, I will do it but with conditions. First, I will put together my own team, and second, we will all get the same cover in the UK that we would have if we were payroll MI6 or 'Five' people. My team will be myself, Maddie my wife, two guys from South Africa called Richard and Ox – you can do all the checks on both of them. I also want two Brits called Jackie Stewart and Handy Andy and our assistant, Michelle Bolt, will have to be partly in the game."

"I'm not sure we can do that. We were planning on providing your team ourselves."

"No deal, either I work with my guys or not at all."

Ros looked hard at Gerald and realised he was absolutely serious. "OK, I will try" and then in some exasperation, "What or who the hell is Handy Andy? I presume you don't also mean the one time champion racing driver?"

"Handy Andy is my own tech person, great with IT and an excellent photographer and cameraman, who builds his own kit for all sorts of eavesdropping. Jackie Stewart is a nickname for a man who can make cars do things that should only happen in films, and is also the safest, fastest driver I know."

"Hmm, that sounds as if you don't have much faith in our people?"

"I didn't say that, but two different types of teams in the field should mean we get everything."

Gerald raised his glass, Ros picked hers up and they clinked before ending the business part of the meal with Ros saying, "OK, if I can get you what you want it's a deal. They did warn me you could be a pain in the neck. We are not often in a situation like this, Gerald, really ahead of the game. This could be the Service's biggest win for ages."

By the time Gerald had finished telling Maddie the whole story of his meeting with Ros, they were nearly back home in Bude, having just passed the Deer Park Nursing Home on the outskirts of Holsworthy.

Maddie was not actually keen on getting involved in Ros's operation because she felt it was all too close to home. However, subject to Ros getting agreement to his requests Gerald had said he would do it, and she knew it would be a waste of time to argue. She did have one question, "Are we doing this for king and country or are we being paid?"

"Definitely paid. Once Ros has agreed, I will tell her how much I want for each of our team; then when that is fixed I will contact everyone."

"Well, that's good. This can pay for our planned trip to the Antarctic; also we need a change of vehicle, and apparently in the Kalahari Buks has modified the shape of the Kalahari Gold school bus, so they need a new one."

"OK, done. I will work all that out and that can be our fee."

Not for the first time Gerald marvelled at the speed with

which Maddie could allocate money, it was almost as if she had a permanent list in her mind of what was needed next!

MI6 very often paid its outside help in cash which Gerald thought would be attractive to his team. After dinner later that night Gerald thought about what payments he should ask for his team. He decided to base the fees on a minimum of four weeks' work, irrespective of whether the job took that long or not, and then if it took longer, there would be a weekly rate thereafter. Gerald had given Ros his two conditions and there was now nothing more he could do until he heard from her.

Later in bed while he waited for sleep his thoughts were on Igor Petrov. What was being proposed was almost a sting operation which had great appeal for him. If it came off it would achieve a serious double whammy: recruit a well-placed new agent and embarrass the hell out of Putin and his Kremlin thugs. If Igor chose to tell all, embarrass his past masters and defect, that would not be the ultimate double whammy that Ros wanted, because she would have liked him to go back to Moscow and work for MI6 as a double agent. However, he had genuinely liked Igor and exposing Moscow and giving Igor and his family a new life in the West would still be a great result. He was half looking forward to meeting Igor again and wondered just how difficult and dangerous things might get before they next met.

4

Moscow, 2024

Igor Petrov had enjoyed the power and authority that came with being a senior officer in the GRU. He was making much more money now as a private intelligence operator than he had been when he was a government employee, but the money didn't wholly make up for the loss of recognised official status. When he eventually stopped working he wanted to be rich, and so making money was now his main focus. He sometimes indulged in a dangerous fantasy and wondered how much he could get from the Americans if he went to work for them as a double agent.

Since the end of the Union of Soviet Socialist Republics (USSR) Petrov had found himself slowly but surely becoming less of a Russian patriot than he had once been. He had been regularly transferring surplus money to a small discreet bank in Vienna. When and if he thought he had built up sufficient funds he intended to look seriously at moving to the West. His years with the GRU watching operations and conducting his own had given him lots of experience with false identities, how to melt into different societies and disappear. He was convinced that he had perfected an accent which would enable him to pass as an east coast middle-class American, although an expert in dialects would be more likely to fix him as coming from Toronto in Canada. Igor was not aware that his accent was more Canadian than east coast American, but ironically, when he thought of a possible move to the West it was Canada that came to mind rather than the USA.

His friendship with Yevgeny Prigozhin, the one-time boss of the Wagner mercenary group, had resulted in him and his close circle of associates being offered regular lucrative work for the FSB and the SVR. However, for the last couple of years of his life, before the plane he was on mysteriously blew up in the sky, Prigozhin's relationship with the FSB and other organisations of the Russian State had become increasingly tense and often hostile. This had not adversely affected Igor who now often worked directly for the SVR, the FSB and the Main Intelligence Directorate (GRU).

A month ago he had been called in by the FSB and the SVR and briefed on an assignment to be conducted against the British. The officer who briefed him had a wry smile on his face as he explained that Igor was already familiar with the target area. He was being asked to go to North Cornwall where many years before he had been shark fishing with Gerald. Igor remembered seeing the GCHQ satellite dishes on the cliffs north of Bude and remembered being surprised that there was no obviously visible security presence on the water guarding the sea approach to the intelligence-gathering station. His assumption had been that land-based radar was closely monitoring the sea approaches, which he thought probably explained the lack of naval or coastguard patrol vessels.

His guess was only partially correct. In fact, the GCHQ station is not only guarded by dedicated radar specifically watching the sea approaches, there is also a range of other measures keeping an eye on the sea, air and land areas surrounding GCHQ. A large unidentified foreign vessel approaching the coast would undoubtedly be interdicted, interrogated and destroyed if appropriate. Radio signal jamming, satellite surveillance and land patrols are also in continual operation.

During the briefing Igor remembered his surprise at the

apparent lack of defensive security because it would now be a feature of how this new proposed operation would be planned. Satellite surveillance by the Russians had noted the frequent presence of small local fishing vessels close to the GCHQ station. From what the Russians could see it would be easy to approach the site on a small fishing boat, and launch a number of shoulder-fired missiles or drones at the dishes and buildings which would destroy the site's capabilities. One of Igor's first tasks after arriving in the UK would be to conduct a couple of dummy run approaches from the sea to test the viability of the plan.

Crooklets Beach in Bude is 4.2 miles south of GCHQ at Cleave Camp, and very few of those swimming, surfing and sunbathing on Crooklets are aware that underneath the beach sand a cable goes out to sea, crossing the Atlantic Ocean to North America. The cable belongs to Google and carries a large proportion of the United Kingdom's transatlantic internet communications. At the briefing it was explained to Igor that if the GCHQ satellite station was attacked, and at the same time the undersea cable was sabotaged, a severe blow would be dealt to the UK's communications. Remedial measures would be taken quickly, but the UK's reputation and prestige would be damaged. News of the attacks would be widely publicised around the world, and the British people would be made to feel very vulnerable.

The Russian intelligence services had several months ago created a bogus Islamic extremist organisation with a readily accessible online presence, but otherwise nothing physical could be found. The Islamic People's Front (IPF) was created by the SVR for use when an opportunity arose. The operation for which Igor Petrov was being briefed would be a perfect fit for the non-existent terrorist organisation. Igor was told to recruit Syrians for the operation, and as soon as the attacks occurred, the IPF would acknowledge responsibility and claim it had been carried out as a reprisal for British support for Israel during the Israeli/Gaza war which started on October 7th, 2023 when Hamas launched attacks into southern Israel.

The Russians did not expect Western intelligence agencies to be fooled for long, but the use of Syrians and the IPF claim would muddy the waters and assist in making the attacks deniable for the Russians. It was vital to the Russians to have deniability to avoid being blamed for attacking a NATO country as this could lead the world's two largest nuclear powers towards a confrontation which would threaten the whole of humanity.

Although he was no longer in government service, and therefore technically could not be ordered to accept the assignment, in Putin's Russia people like Igor recognised that survival, making money and having a good standard of living all meant staying on the right side of the State. He had been offered a substantial budget, and although he would have to explain expenditure he could more or less draw funds as he wanted and needed them.

The size of his own fee would be agreed on once he had formally accepted the assignment. He did not think of Magd Dossari as a close friend, but he had been an associate and often a colleague for many years. Igor did not trust Dossari an inch, but knew he would be utterly reliable as long as it was in his interest to be so.

Dossari's Syrian and Iranian connections could be invaluable and pre-dated the Russo-Ukrainian War which had seen Iran supply huge numbers of drones and other military equipment to Russia. He had all the right connections in the shady world of illegal under-the-radar arms dealing in the Middle East, and would be the perfect person to procure men, weapons and explosives for the non-existent Islamic group to use in its attacks in the UK. To further the illusion the Russians would lay weapons procurement trails which would end with the IPF, and Western agencies would be fed leads which also pointed to the IPF.

Several years before when Igor was still in the First Main Directorate (ex-GRU), Magd Dossari had popped up on his radar in Kyrgystan, or more correctly, the Kyrgyz Republic. Kyrgyzstan declared independence from the Soviet Union when it collapsed in 1991. However, the Russians kept a close eye on former USSR states, including Kyrgystan, and for a while this was Igor Petrov's responsibility. On visits to Bishkek, Kyrgystan's capital, Igor often came across the name Magd Dossari, and on one occasion watched him in a Bishkek casino playing roulette surrounded by girls – who Igor decided were hookers or chancers – and ordering champagne as if it were cheap mineral water. Igor had asked a member of casino staff who the high rolling gambler was, and was told it was a Syrian Arab sheikh called Magd Dossari. Magd was not really a sheikh, but he quite liked the deference and did not correct anyone using the title. Igor had introduced himself and asked Magd to meet him for lunch the next day.

Something about Dossari's demeanour intrigued Igor and he spent the morning before the lunch finding out all he could about the Syrian.

Dossari was forty-three years old, and came from a respected middle-class family with a home in Damascus and a summer holiday property on the Mediterranean coast near Latakia. Magd's father, Mahmoud, had been a general practice doctor who had always been careful to keep his family on the right side of the Al Assad family who had ruled Syria and its Baath Party for decades, before being finally ousted by rebel factions.

President Hafez al Assad had been a staunch ally of the USSR, and after succeeding his father, Bashar al Assad, continued to be a close friend of Russia to where he and his family fled when his rule collapsed. When he was nineteen years old Magd Dossari joined the elite Republican Guard, and some years later he came to the attention of General Maher al Assad, the Guard's commander. In a skirmish with Israeli troops near the occupied Golan Heights Captain Dossari had found himself close to the general, and had hustled him to safety, firing at the Israelis as they moved away.

Captain Magd Dossari was promoted to the rank of major the day after the action and became one of the General's closest and most trusted aides serving as his personal bodyguard, friend and advisor. They shared an appetite for very young women and often satisfied their desires together, changed partners and enjoyed swapping opinions after the girls had been dismissed. The girls were procured from as far away as Morocco and the identities of the two men were always carefully protected. Fear and money assured the girls' silence which was as well because violence resulting in injury was not unknown in the sex sessions. If anything, Captain Magd was more violent than the General, and more than once young women had ended up in hospital with serious injuries which needed medical treatment.

By the time Magd left the army he was thirty-five years old and was a lieutenant colonel. He was a good shot with handguns and rifles, and was a martial arts student who kept himself physically very fit. His friendship with Major General Maher al Assad was widely acknowledged, both in Syria and in related countries like Russia, Iran, and the Russian satellites. Since becoming a civilian Magd had used his contacts and influence to become a very successful arms dealer. His addiction to adrenalin was satisfied by taking various well-paid assignments as a mercenary.

The lunch in Bishkek was cordial and relaxed but each man realised he was being sized up and evaluated by the other. Igor was due to retire from the GRU a few months later, and had already decided to continue in intelligence and related fields as a private enterprise operator. He saw Dossari as being a potentially valuable future contact and colleague. His instincts had been correct, and he and Magd had developed a close working relationship which remained on a professional level rather than becoming a personal friendship. Each man knew that they came from a world in which trust was based on self-interest.

After his joint FSB/SVR briefing Igor called Magd and was happy to discover he was in Moscow. Nothing was said on the phone except the details of where they would meet the following evening. Igor didn't trust either the cell phone network or landlines. He wanted to put a proposition to his colleague, and didn't want to run even the slightest risk of what he was going to put to Magd somehow leaking to a listener.

They met on the bank of the Moskva River, and during their long walk before dinner Igor explained the British operation. After Magd had agreed to join Igor, he tasked him with recruiting two teams of Arab mercenaries, each of three men. He stressed that two of the members of one team should be qualified and experienced scuba divers.

After their walk they went for dinner. They continued discussing the new operation but because they both now knew what was involved they were able to talk safely in general terms without mentioning names and specifics. They agreed that this assignment was the biggest thing either of them had ever tackled, and because they were working without any diplomatic accreditation, they knew they would spend the rest of their lives in a British jail if they were caught. For this reason they decided to insist on much larger than usual payments so that their future in Russia, Syria, or elsewhere, if they so chose, would be financially secure and safe.

Igor and Magd were both rich men, but being involved in attacks on a NATO country, responsibility for which would be denied by Russia, and claimed by a non-existent organisation, would propel them into the super league of the world's most hunted men and even more money would be needed to buy anonymity.

The Americans had hunted Osama Bin Laden for ten years until they found and killed him. The Brits weren't the Americans, but the intelligence agencies and police forces of every NATO country would have them on their most wanted lists.

Another consideration was that if the Russians could be proved to be behind the attacks, it would be an act of war committed against a NATO country. For this reason both Igor and Magd knew that if it became expedient, the Russians would kill them rather than run any risk of Russian involvement being exposed. The stakes were high and the dangers very real, so the payments had to be high. Each man decided to insist on a fee of five million dollars paid outside Russia or Syria. Igor had been told that the attacks were to happen in late June or early July, and they agreed that that time frame would be viable.

It was an abnormally warm early May evening when they parted company outside the restaurant. They had two months to put everything together and agreed to meet regularly during the process and avoid electronic communication as much as possible. Igor told Magd that he would negotiate the payments for them and the team and would inform Magd as soon as he could confirm that their financial demands would be met.

Since his briefing Igor had often wondered whether during his upcoming time in Britain, and especially in North Cornwall, he might bump into his old "friend" Gerald Richmond. During his briefing he had been told that Gerald regularly appeared in the files of the various Russian intelligence directorates, and while there was no actual conclusive proof that Gerald worked for British Intelligence it was strongly suspected. Intelligence agencies don't like coincidences, and Russian intelligence did not think that Gerald's approach to Igor all those years ago was for the reasons Gerald had pretended.

Nevertheless, Igor had liked Gerald, and still clearly remembered his weekend in Cornwall and his day shark fishing. In the lounge of his home there was a framed photograph of Igor with his porbeagle shark, which had been taken by Gerald, framed and given to Igor as a present.

At home in bed that night with his wife Svetlana asleep beside him Igor listened to her breathing and realised that if the operation succeeded and provided the opportunity to leave Russia he wanted his family with him in his new life. He decided he would carefully sound out his wife's attitude to living in the West and if it was positive he would start planting the seeds. Both sets of their parents had died and they really had nothing to keep them in Russia other than their two sons. It was several hours before Igor fell into a troubled sleep.

5

Gerald got a call from Ros three days after Igor had his joint briefing from the FSB and the SVR. On a personal level Gerald and Maddie liked the month of May in the UK, as it was a bridge between spring and summer. When the weather was good in Cornwall, the countryside, beaches and cliffs could be enjoyed without the holiday crowds that would come later.

On a business or professional level Gerald thought that May could be a pain in the neck, because two Mondays were Bank Holidays, and this often played havoc with business appointments. It had become common practice for people to take the Friday off when the Mondays were Bank Holidays, and for this and various other reasons it meant that Gerald and Ros were not able to meet until nine days after her call to Gerald. All Ros would say on the phone was that Gerald's requests had got the green light. She now wanted to meet face to face to take the whole project forward including agreeing fees for Gerald's team.

Once again Gerald travelled to London and the pair met at Rules. Gerald agreed to realistic but generous fees for his team and for himself and Maddie. MI6 liked making these types of payments in cash; so Gerald and Ros agreed a schedule of part payments which would be delivered as the operation went along and then paid in small amounts over a period so as not to create interest at banks suspicious of cash. Gerald was told the same as Igor had been by his Moscow masters, which was that within reason, and provided it could be justified, he could spend whatever was necessary.

It obviously greatly amused Ros to be indirectly employing people called Handy Andy and Jackie Stewart because she continued to refer to them on several occasions.

Before they parted company they went to a Pakistani mobile phone shop and Ros bought four burner phones, two for each of them. They would each call out from one phone and receive calls on the other. Burner phones are in common use by criminals, spies and others who need phones which can't be traced, are not listed anywhere and are unlikely to be listened to. Cheap non-internet phones are bought and then discarded regularly to be replaced by the next burner. It is thought they are called burners because they are "burned" or discarded regularly.

The next step would be for Gerald to enlist his team and get them all to London; they agreed this should be done within three weeks. There was little flexibility in this time frame because the MI6 Moscow source had recently reported that Igor and his Russian Intelligence employers were into their planning phase, and Igor and some ex-Syrian army mercenaries would arrive in Britain in late May or early June. Gerald's team plus MI6 field agents, trainers and technical experts would all move into Tiverton Castle in Devon where all the self-catering accommodation had been rented for two months. The castle would serve as a training base and then a field headquarters and supply base. The owners of Tiverton Castle were Angus and Alison Gordon. The heavy hints that secret work was involved not only appealed to their patriotism, it also guaranteed the silence of the Gordons who were both loyal British subjects.

Tiverton Castle is home to five self-catering units, which could accommodate a total of twenty and offered plenty of flexibility. Gerald and Maddie would have their own accommodation, as would Richard and Ox sharing and Jackie Stewart and Handy Andy sharing. MI6 were sending a husband and wife team to do the cooking and cleaning and keep an eye on security. There would be four others to brief and train Gerald, Maddie and their team, and to keep as close as possible to what the Russians were up to, using electronic means.

Ros and Gerald had agreed that neither Gerald's team nor MI6 personnel would routinely carry firearms; however, one member of the MI6 group would have access to firearms which could in an extreme or unexpected situation be issued to Gerald, Richard or Ox. In normal circumstances if and when armed intervention was needed Ros would use her channels to secure the services of the SAS or another specialist armed unit.

Handy Andy and Jackie Stewart were both UK residents who lived near London. Without knowing what they were getting into they both responded positively when Gerald rang and asked them to meet him for lunch in London so that he could offer them up to two months' interesting work in Britain that summer.

Nothing more was said on the phone and three days later they met in the Paddington Hilton Hotel where Gerald had taken a room for half a day. The trio met in the lobby before going up to the room which Handy Andy immediately swept for listening devices. Nothing was said for a couple of minutes until Andy said, "All clear."

Jackie and Andy had a relationship which involved continual light friendly banter. "What a load of old bollocks! How could anyone know we are here? You just wanted to show off and play with your toys," offered Jackie.

"Well, maybe my toys could save your life one day if you don't first wrap yourself around a tree pretending to be a racing driver," countered Andy.

Gerald grinned inwardly. Some people don't ever change. He knew this pair hadn't seen each other for several months and yet their first verbal exchange probably carried on in exactly the same vein they had left off when last they met.

"I've got a lot to explain and there's plenty to discuss, so sit tight and try not to break your long-standing practice by being civil to each other while I get on to room service and sort out some beer, coffee and sandwiches."

By the time they left the room two hours later Andy and Jackie had all the information which Gerald had from Ros, they had agreed their fees, decided what equipment they would bring and agreed to next meet in Tiverton at the end of May.

Jackie intended to bring a Range Rover, a long wheelbase Land Rover 110 and a souped-up wide-tyre converted VW people carrier van. He couldn't drive three vehicles down from London to Devon, thus he asked Andy to drive the Land Rover so that he only had to do two trips instead of three.

Gerald went downstairs with them to the lobby, and as he watched them cross the road together he mused that there could hardly be two more different characters. Jackie was thirty years old, a fraction over six feet tall and was proud of his dark brown shoulder-length hair. He played guitar in a Bromley-based blues band, but made the main part of his living as a driving instructor.

Gerald and Maddie first met him seven years before when Gerald had bought Maddie an off-road 4WD driving experience as a present and Jackie had been Maddie's instructor. When they returned after four hours uphill and down dale in a short wheelbase Land Rover Maddie was buzzing. They had obviously hit it off, and Maddie kept referring to Jackie as a "raving bloody lunatic" which he clearly took as a compliment and often countered with, "I'm not sure I wouldn't describe you as the same, Lady M."

How the Lady M moniker had come about that day Jackie couldn't remember, but to him she was and always would be Lady M. On four occasions in the last seven years Gerald had hired Jackie, and more than once he had driven Gerald in situations which were sometimes dangerous, and in others, success had been sealed by his extraordinary skills behind the wheel. Gerald was fond of saying, "Everyone thinks they are pretty good drivers until they meet Jackie, then they know what a good driver really is."

Andy sported a neat ginger crew cut, was four inches shorter than Jackie and tended to march rather than walk. He left the British Army after ten years in the Royal Signals and set up his own IT consulting business. He actually liked Jackie, but would never have wanted anyone to know; so he continually referred to him as a sloppy, long-haired layabout hippie who couldn't play the guitar and crashed cars. Jackie's return description was, "Four-eyed ginger geek". As well as anything hi-tech and to do with IT and communications, Andy was also a photographer and a shark nut. Several years before he had volunteered to join one of Gerald's shark research expeditions in the Adriatic. Three expeditions later and Gerald always referred to him as his best ever volunteer.

Gerald and Maddie usually described their adventures and operations as gigs. Andy and Jackie had been on three gigs together and helped each other in more than one sticky situation. Behind the insults and the banter lay a deep mutual respect.

Before calling Andy and Jackie Gerald had made an encrypted internet call to the other two prospective members of the team in South Africa. Richard Matson had been a friend of Gerald and Maddie's for many years; they had recently worked with

Richard and a friend, Tim Oxley, in the Kalahari. That gig had come to a very successful conclusion. Gerald had been impressed not only by how Richard and his friend had worked well together, but also by how they handled themselves in difficult and dangerous situations.

The managers of lodges in places like the Kalahari have to have endless patience and be multiskilled. Dangerous wild animals, snakes, scorpions and sometimes extreme heat are all part of what a lodge manager has to deal with, in addition to looking after guests who can often stretch patience to the limit. As well as all the diverse skills that Richard needed as a lodge manager, he was proficient with firearms, never panicked and could take care of himself and others in dangerous situations. He was just old enough to have been of an age when military service was compulsory in South Africa; so his experience in the army added to his diverse capabilitites.

Everyone who knew Tim Oxley called him Ox. With his hair in a ponytail, Ox was just over two metres (6 ft 6 in) tall, and weighed close to 140 kgs which is about 22 stone. There was no fat making up his weight; the term gentle giant was made for him. Ox had played rugby as number eight in the middle of the second row of the scrum. Both at school and later in club rugby he had played to a good standard and some believed he could have gone on and played professionally for one of South Africa's leading teams. Ox had made a living as a long distance lorry driver, an oil rig roustabout, diver, freelance pilot and mechanic. During the recent gig in the Kalahari he had shown himself as being comfortable handling weapons and unflappable in tight situations, but otherwise was easygoing and ready to turn his hand to anything. Ox and Richard had been a formidable highly effective team, and after working with them in the Kalahari Gerald had made a mental note to use them in future whenever the circumstances were right.

His briefing on the encrypted line to South Africa had not been as full as his in-person meeting with Andy and Jackie, but after only thirty minutes on the phone Richard had said, "Sounds fun," and Ox had added, "I'm in." Gerald said he would transfer funds for air tickets and expenses and would see them at the end of May in Britain.

Years before an Englishman and a Russian had each been trying to recruit the other as a spy. Neither had been made aware of the other's real intentions. Now the old acquaintances were both putting together teams which would soon be locked in a life and death high-stakes clash. Both Gerald and Igor had often wondered what would happen if they ever met again. Neither man could have known that the day would come, nor could they have predicted the circumstances or the life-changing outcome of their next encounter in Cornwall.

6

Moscow 2024

Igor had several lengthy intense meetings with his joint FSB/ SVR controllers in the days following his meeting with Magd. They realised he would have to tell Magd the truth about who they were actually working for but gave him strict instructions to limit the "truth" as much as possible. Igor was further instructed that under no circumstances were Magd's team to be told of Russian involvement. The story had to be that they were all working for the Islamic People's Front who were funding the operation.

They all realised that Magd's people would have never heard of the IPF, and would check and find it seemed to only exist on the internet. The explanation which Igor and Magd would give would be that the IPF was a secret Iranian proxy organisation which had been created specifically to carry out this attack which was in retaliation for Britain's support for Israel in its war on Gaza and attacks on Lebanon.

The paymasters agreed $5,000,000 after each for Igor and Magd and $100,000 for each of Magd's six mercenaries. What Igor was not told was that a two-man SVR hit team would be in Britain for the whole time of the operation, and immediately after the two attacks had been carried out, both Igor and Magd would be assassinated by their own side. The Russians realised that the Western intelligence agencies would likely quickly see through the screen of IPF being the attackers, and would initially suspect Iran, but ultimately would conclude the Russians were responsible. This did not concern Moscow, in fact, it suited them because it enhanced Moscow's image to its allies, however, it was vital that Russian involvement would never be able to be proved to avoid the consequences of having launched a direct attack on a NATO country.

Any possibility that either Igor or Magd might be caught and interrogated, or would ever talk to anyone about the operation, had to be eliminated. Very simply, this meant they both had to be silenced, permanently.

Magd's six men were not brought to Moscow, instead Igor and Magd flew to Damascus and spent two days running through the basics of the operation without identifying what specific target they would be attacking. The men were all professionals who understood the way the covert world worked. They were told that they would soon receive air tickets to fly to Doha where they would be fully briefed and issued with new identities and tickets to their final destination.

Magd told the men to tell their family and friends they would be away for about a month and during that time would not be in contact. The men were not told at that time that when they were met in Doha their cell phones, laptops and other devices would be left there and then sent back to Damascus where they would reclaim them once the job was done. They were also not told that once in London they would be given burner phones which made and received calls but did not have internet access nor allow overseas calls. Igor was working on the principle that until they were in Doha and fully briefed on the eve of their departure to London the less they knew the better.

The operation was discussed in general terms and the seabed targets were described first. It was decided to keep things as simple as possible, using high explosive charges with timer switches and back-up switches to destroy the undersea cable. The explosives would be laid by two divers and set to go off after two hours to give the men time to get clear of the area. The three men in this team were all experienced seamen. They would buy a boat locally and crew it themselves posing as a wreck-diving group on holiday in the UK. Once the divers had set the charges and were back on the surface the team would steam out to sea where they would be met by an ocean-going fishing vessel.

The Irish-flagged vessel had been sourced by the SVR some weeks before and had been chartered for the whole period. The first job would be to deliver crates at sea off the Cornish coast to the attack teams. The vessel would then steam off several miles and stand by while fishing. The second part of the task of the chartered vessel would be to rendevouz at sea with Magd's two teams after the attacks, when they would scuttle their boats. The SVR had taken a lot of trouble finding a vessel with a mixed crew which had a reputation for being part-time smugglers and not being over particular about the type of work they did. The crew were being very well paid and were unlikely to be overly curious about what they were doing.

The second team would attack the satellite dishes from the sea using either drones, shoulder-fired RPG weapons or missiles. Rockets or missiles would be fired by all three men who, depending on circumstances at the time, would each fire two or three which would only take a few minutes. The rockets would not completely destroy the GCHQ installation but would certainly affect functionality in a major way for a considerable time. The other option was to use drones carrying explosives. The aircraft would be flown into the targets and the explosives detonated. The decision whether to use RPG missiles or drones would be made after the teams had done a reconnaisance of the target from the sea. The Irish vessel would be carrying drones, rockets and missiles, and the attack team would dump whatever equipment they didn't want to use over the side and into the sea. The Russian belief was that the very fact that a successful attack had been mounted against a leading NATO country would expose the vulnerability of the West.

The broad plan had been agreed, but the detail would wait until the teams got into the UK and were able to conduct a detailed reconnaisance on the ground and evaluate all the facts.

The team of mercenaries had now taken shape and had a basic mission plan. What Igor and his paymasters didn't know was that MI6 had a source which would keep the British ahead of the game and allow them to match and pre-empt Russian moves. The other unknown for Igor was that his team of freelance mercenaries would soon be up against another team led by an old acquaintance of his.

AUTHOR'S NOTE: When Ivor Petrov left Russia and journeyed to the UK he did so under a new identity using the name Dimitry Volkov with his documents describing him as an "Investment Consultant". To avoid confusion I will continue using the name Igor Petrov.

7

Ox took an internal flight from Cape Town to Johannesburg, where Richard joined him and together they boarded a British Airways flight to London. Neither man was overly keen on night flights because even in business class, with seats that went flat and became beds it was difficult to get a good night's sleep. They landed on time at London's Heathrow Airport and walked out of British Airways Terminal 5 just after 07:30 and found Maddie waiting for them.

"This is a much better-looking chauffeur than I was expecting," Richard quipped loudly to Ox. Maddie was wearing a huge grin as her friends walked towards her and as Richard had intended, she overheard his remark to Ox.

"Really, Sir, flattery always works. I hope it will be reflected in my tip." She held her arms wide for hugs and continued, "Now come and say hello properly, you pair of old scoundrels."

On the drive west she apologised that Gerald had not been at the airport to meet them and explained that he had a long-standing arrangement to go hiking with an old friend on Exmoor, looking for red deer. Maddie pointed out landmarks along their route down the M4 towards Bristol and answered lots of questions about Tiverton Castle, Handy Andy and Jackie Stewart. She was amused that her two South African friends seemed far more interested in the idea of staying in a castle and who they would be working with, than in the operation they would be part of.

At Bristol she turned onto the M5 heading south-west and just over an hour later left the motorway at Junction 27 on the last leg to Tiverton. They had stopped at a services while on the M5, and after buying coffee and croissants, headed for the petrol pumps where Maddie filled up her Range Rover. When Richard and Ox saw Maddie filling her own petrol tank they couldn't resist taking photos on their cell phones to send to friends in South Africa, where no one ever had to fill their own vehicles because there were always attendants to do it for you. For at least the next ten minutes Maddie had to put up with being ribbed by false sympathy expressed at her having to fill her own tank and listen to how Britain must be in a terrible state if petrol stations couldn't afford to hire attendants!

They arrived at Tiverton Castle just after midday, and as they got out of the vehicle, were greeted by Tom and Fiona Edworthy. The Edworthys had worked for MI6 for many years, doing what they called hosting jobs. Tom Edworthy had come to the attention of MI6 when the Service was looking for a bodyguard to shepherd and protect a young Arab prince while he was in the UK at university. The prince's father was an MI6 contact and believed his son would be an abduction risk. Tom was working for a private company called Shield Limited which employed ex-military personnel, mainly past members of the SAS, the SBS or the Paras who acted as bodyguards, military advisors, and training officers for a variety of individuals and governments around the world.

Tom had become a close friend of the prince and once that job was finished MI6 recruited him for other similar assignments. Tom and Fiona's role as security guards and housekeepers had started when another well known Arab royal family had taken a castle in Scotland for a month's holiday one summer and needed a security guard and a cook/housekeeper. At that time Fiona was running a small bed and breakfast operation out of their house in Hastings, and so Tom was approached to see if he and his wife would take the job as a couple working for the Arab family for their stay in the Highlands.

Providing housekeepers and bodyguards was not normally something that MI6 would get involved in, but as with the first Arab prince, the family's father had a working connection with MI6. The job had gone very well and had led to Tom and Fiona being employed to work together as a couple, either running serviced safe houses, or providing base facilities when MI6 officers were working in the field in groups.

At Tiverton Castle Fiona, assisted by a local girl who had been proposed by the castle owners, would provide cooking, laundry and cleaning services for Gerald and Maddie, their team and the MI6 personnel. Tom would make himself useful whenever needed, and would keep an eye on security in case the group's presence attracted attention, or the opposition somehow found out where they were and tried to compromise them.

Fiona had already allocated accommodation to all those staying at the castle. Gerald and Maddie were given Pear Tree which was the only apartment for a couple alone, Richard and Ox had a bedroom each in Upper South Court, as did Handy Andy and Jackie Stewart in Lower East Court. The Edworthys were in Castle Lodge with a spare bedroom, and the four MI6 personnel would be in Castle Barton which was the largest apartment with a dining room, sitting room, study and three bedrooms. Fiona had picked Castle Barton as the apartment where the whole group could work together when having training, briefing, or conference sessions, and which would also serve as the mess for meals.

Gerald and Maddie had arrived a few nights before, and soon after they had settled in, Fiona took them on a tour of all five apartments while explaining to Maddie what she described as the rooming arrangements. Fiona sailed ahead talking to

Maddie as they walked while completely ignoring Gerald. Gerald wondered whether Fiona was one of those women who thought that by and large most men were blithering idiots who needed guiding by women – when they had time. Later he mentioned to Tom that his wife seemed a competent and commanding sort of person and Tom looked at him, gave him a wink, burst out laughing and said, "You noticed, did you, Boss?"

After the handshakes and introductions Fiona told Richard and Ox they were in Upper South Court and suggested they unpack and settle in. Richard hid a smile as he couldn't help thinking that they had just been given an order and then dismissed. Tom helped with their bags as they headed for the impressive old wooden door which led to their apartment.

As they walked away, almost as an afterthought, Fiona said to their departing backs, "The other two lunatics left the Land Rover here and have gone by train to collect two more cars. They will be back around midnight; so you will meet them tomorrow and Gerald should be back any minute."

The reference to lunatics caused Richard and Ox to exchange a glance which Tom noticed and quietly remarked, "Fiona has her own way of talking, you'll soon get used to it."

Later that afternoon Ros arrived with three members of MI6 in a Volkswagen Campervan with blacked-out windows. Ros did not plan to be present in Tiverton for the duration of the operation; so had brought Christine, her assistant, to act as liaison when she was away.

Sometimes words exactly fit the people they are describing. William and Henry were both geeks and talked like geeks using a vocabulary that non-geeks often couldn't understand. Looking at them Maddie estimated they were both about thirty years old. Apart from their confusing use of the English language being of the same age was where any similarity ended.

Henry was over six feet tall, slim, had shoulder-length blonde hair, and looked very fit, which he actually was due to being a keen runner. William had dark hair, was six inches shorter than Henry and had a chocolate addiction which probably explained why he was as plump as Henry was slim.

The VW campervan contained William and Henry's equipment. Their job would be to electronically monitor the activities of Igor's group as closely as possible. They would try to bug them using equipment which would allow them to monitor and intercept emails, cell phone traffic, radio traffic and record what was being said when the Arabs were talking among themselves.

Richard, Ox, Andy and Jackie would form a group which would physically shadow Igor and his people. Because they had previously met Igor, Gerald and Maddie would stay close to the action during surveillance but one step back and out of sight. To a degree the activities of Handy Andy and the two MI6 electronics people would complement each other and might overlap; so they would liaise closely and continually.

Gerald returned in the late afternoon, and that evening Fiona prepared dinner for eight plus herself and her husband. Everyone ate together in Castle Barton where chairs had been brought from the other apartments to convert the dining room into a mess hall and briefing room. The dining room table sat six people comfortably, eight at a push and ten if the chairs made a loose circle around the table with two eating off their laps. Fiona and Tom shuttled between the kitchen and the dining room, and joined the circle to eat off their laps once all the food was on the table.

Gerald had declared that dinner would be a work-free zone,

so the upcoming operation was not discussed. After dinner Gerald and Ros each gave short introductory briefings which finished with Gerald saying that breakfast would be at eight and then, with Andy and Jackie present, there would be a full briefing at nine.

Richard and Ox who were feeling the effects of having flown overnight from South Africa, excused themselves and headed for bed. Maddie produced a pack of cards and a huge jar of one and two pence pieces.

"OK, how about some cards before bed and I will fleece the lot of you."

Maddie didn't know it but William was a mathemetician who also liked to gamble. He smiled and responded, "Well, let's see who fleeces whom!"

Very soon all eight players around the table were engrossed in a game of poker playing with coins which had been shared out by Maddie. It didn't take long before it became obvious that some were better players than others and were taking the game more seriously. Fiona feigned enthusiasm but clearly thought playing poker was really rather silly and soon left the table. For most of the time Maddie and William were locked in a series of almost private contests. No one stayed up late and by the end of the session it was Maddie and William who had accumulated the largest piles of coins to return to the jar.

While those in Tiverton Castle slept, in Qatar's capital Doha, two hours ahead and 3200 miles away by air, Igor and Magd were also asleep. The next day they would prepare for the arrival of Magd's men who would fly in the day after for a day of briefings, before the group members would fly separately to London.

Igor had decided that once he had been paid for this operation he would retire and move somewhere he could buy a boat and spend his life game fishing. He felt settled and relaxed, all he had to do was pull this assignment off.

He would not have been so relaxed had he known he was flying into a trap that would change his life completely, but not in the way he was hoping and planning. Magd had also been thinking about life after the current operation, but in his case he was dreaming of a long holiday spent with an endless stream of young women.

8

Magd Dossari had had no difficulty finding and recruiting the six men who would make up his team. All six men were ex-Syrian army. Three of them had served with Magd in the Republican Guard, the two divers were friends he had often gone diving with and were ex-Syrian navy divers. All six men had worked for Magd before on various private enterprise mercenary operations.

The six Syrians flew separately from Damascus to Doha and went in six taxis from Hamad International Airport to the Sheraton Hotel. Igor had given strict instructions that during their travels to Britain they would never be seen together as a group. In addition to bedrooms he had taken a large two bedroom suite. This would be where the group met during the day they spent in Doha before flying on to London. New identity documents were provided and the other ID documents and anything else that identified the men were left in Doha. All the genuine passports and other items would be hand-carried back to Damascus to await the return of the men after their mission.

The briefings previously given in Damascus were repeated and expanded on. Igor and Magd were very careful never to mention Russian involvement. The IPF was often referred to but the reality was that the Syrians weren't really very interested in the identity of their ultimate paymasters as long as they got paid. Half of their agreed fees were paid electronically in front of them by Igor to their accounts when they were in the Doha hotel, and the other half would be paid as soon as the mission had been carried out.

Igor had obtained British diving and sea angling magazines, and had printed off lots of information from the internet regarding wreck diving off Cornwall. There was also lots of information on sea angling for that team. It covered not just the fish species which would be their supposed quarry, but also technical details about types of fishing rods and reels they would use. Neither the divers nor the anglers needed to be experts on the local aspects of their chosen holiday sport, but they did need to be able to convince casual observers that they were genuine.

Although heavily accented all six men spoke good English and fully understood conversations spoken at normal speed. Their accents and their so obviously being foreign would give them a get-out if their sea angling or local diving knowledge was ever faulted. They would simply claim they hadn't understood what was being said.

The two teams were supposed to be going to Britain on holiday and each group of three would travel together to London, and then head for the Marble Arch Edgeware Road district where reservations had been made for each team in different hotels. Igor and Magd would travel together and on arrival in London would stay at Marble Arch's Cumberland Hotel. Igor would have no contact with the Russian Embassy or any Russian organisation while in Britain, but would communicate regularly with his Moscow controllers via secure links which would change frequently.

One night would be spent in London and then the three groups would travel in three cars to Bovey Castle in Devon which would be their base of operations. The day after flying in the two teams of three and Igor and Magd would go back to Heathrow Airport to pick up the three rental cars which had been reserved for them.

Igor and Magd flew to London on Qatar Airways and arrived late in the afternoon on a bright sunny May day. Among those watching their arrival were two Russian agents. Yevgeny and Alexei watched the pair leave the Terminal Four building and head for the taxi rank. They were SVR killers and their assignment was to either kill Igor and Magd or arrange a fatal accident for them once the operation was over. They had been instructed to keep constant but careful and distant surveillance of their targets. Igor and Magd were trained and experienced operators who would spot surveillance that most people would miss.

The Russian killers watched both men get into a taxi. They were now satisfied that they had seen enough of their targets to be able to recognise them under any circumstances. They couldn't follow Igor and Magd and didn't need to, because they had been informed by Moscow that within a couple of days they would head for Bovey Castle. They had researched Bovey Castle and realised that its remote location meant that if they were to keep eyes on their targets they would also have to stay in the castle complex. This would simultaneously make Alexei and Yevgeny's job both easier and more challenging. However, because Igor would keep in contact with Moscow, and Moscow would feed information to its killers, there would be no risk of completely losing Igor and Magd, so they would be able to work a much looser surveillance.

Normally the SVR would not have deployed their killers so early. They would have waited until the end of the operation. However, no date had been fixed for the attack on the undersea cable and the GCHQ installion. There was no way to be sure of the date of the attack until Igor, Magd and their teams were in place, had done all the necessary reconnaisance, and had rendezvoused with the Irish ship to get the weapons and explosives. It was acknowledged that this would take several days and maybe even a couple of weeks.

Once everything was ready Igor's orders were to carry out the attacks as soon as possible and leave the UK. Igor and Magd would not be at sea with the teams when the attacks were carried out; so would not be with them when they escaped on the Irish fishing vessel. They would despatch their men to carry out the attacks, and would then wait ashore in Bude until they knew the attacks had been carried out before driving straight to Heathrow Airport and flying out of the UK.

Events could unfold very fast, and the only way to be sure that Yevgeny and Alexei would be near enough to Igor and Magd to be able to carry out the assassinations at short notice would be for them to be close enough to react fast as soon as the attacks had happened.

After checking in at the Cumberland Hotel Igor and Magd went in search of a shop selling cheap simple mobile phones. They made enquiries at a shop in the Edgeware Road and were recommended to another shop in Praed Street near to Paddington Railway Station. They wanted to buy two burner phones for each member of the group, so needed sixteen.

The owner of the shop was a Pakistani who responded very favourably when Magd walked in and said, "As-Salaam-Alaikum." He didn't try to continue in Arabic because that would have probably registered with the shop owner and been remembered. A large amount of cash was handed over and twenty minutes later Igor and Magd left with their phones.

The next day the whole group travelled back to Heathrow to

collect their hire cars and then headed west on the M4. They all stopped at the Leigh Delamere Services where Igor handed out the phones and they took note of each others numbers.

Three holiday lodges had been rented at Bovey Castle for two weeks, and at the services Igor repeated the part of his earlier briefings which dealt with their arrival at the hotel. The supposed sea anglers would be staying in one house, the divers in another and Igor and Magd in a third. The anglers and the divers were all Syrian, but were actually all travelling on Lebanese passports. They were clearly all Arabs, so it made sense for them all to be staying as one group on holiday.

Fishing rods, wetsuits, masks and other equipment would all be bought locally in the first couple of days of their stay. Not only was the equipment necessary for their tasks but leaving it lying around in their lodges helped to support their cover stories.

The divers planned to visit Aquanaut in Exeter and the Teign Diving Centre in Teignmouth. They had researched both shops, and were confident that between the two shops they would be able to buy all they needed. The anglers had found shops in Brixham and Torquay, but didn't want to stand out as novices, so had decided to book a couple of days at sea with a charter angling boat to get experience. They had all held rods and been fishing before so were not complete beginners, nevertheless, their lack of experience might get them noticed, so they aimed to limit this risk. Igor and Magd would check in together after the other two groups; their cover was that of two real estate investors looking for properties for clients from the Gulf. They had chosen a row of three lodges together called the C lodges, Cleve Tor, Cox Tor and Claret Tor. The three lodges were only a short walk from the car park in which all the vehicles belonging to lodge guests had to be parked, and the hotel's main building was also a very short walk from their lodges.

Each lodge had three bedrooms and was capable of sleeping up to eight. The check-in for the lodges was not in the main hotel building, it was at a building called East Lodge which served all lodge guests.

Igor had decided they would arrive on a Friday evening because this was likely to be the busiest night of the week for people checking into the lodges for weekend breaks. The two groups of Syrians checked in first half an hour apart. Igor watched the second group turn into the Bovey Castle gate; then remained parked on the road for nearly an hour while he watched eleven other vehicles turn in. He hoped that at least two or three of these vehicles would head for East Lodge to check in which would break up their arrival into the three C lodges and therefore draw less attention to them.

Within a couple of days the hotel staff and guests would get used to seeing Igor's party together, but he wanted their knowing each other to appear to evolve naturally. Each lodge cost £5,000 per week. Igor reckoned that seven Arabs all arriving at once and knowing each and taking lodges next door to each other would be a talking point among hotel staff. He hoped that his attempts at blurring this picture would lower their profile and reduce curiosity.

After dinner on the night they checked in Igor sent a coded message to Moscow confirming their arrival. Half an hour later Moscow had told Yevgeny and Alexei where the group was staying. The assassins knew that it would take Igor at least a few days to be ready to mount the attacks; so when they made their online reservations for rooms in the hotel part of Bovey Castle they timed their arrival for three days later.

That evening, by prior arrangement, Magd happened to bump into his six men in the bar before dinner. For the benefit of the staff and other guests Magd made a great show of hearing Arabic being spoken which triggered him to loudly and very obviously introduce himself to his fellow Levantine Arabs. This piece of theatre meant that, although when they arrived they had pretended not to know each other, Magd and his friend Igor would now have every reason to be friendly with, and be seen with, the six Syrian mercenaries.

9

When Gerald and Maddie came down to breakfast they found Andy and Jackie already at the table.

Andy spoke first, "Morning Boss, morning Maddie." Jackie added, "Boss, Lady M." Richard and Ox were next to appear and arrived as Fiona was bringing boxes of cereals, milk, sugar and other items to the sideboard by the table.

Her, "Morning everyone," seemed friendly enough but she was almost wearing a scowl which said, "You lot are early, I wasn't quite ready!"

Gerald introduced Andy and Jackie to Ox and Richard, and the conversation immediately went to vehicles when Ox asked Jackie questions about his modified VW van parked outside. With its darkened windows, wide wheels, fat tyres, radio aerials and satellite dishes the vehicle looked like something out of the famous American TV series the *A-Team*. In addition to the visible modifications Jackie had had the suspension slightly raised and hardened to give the VW a degree of off-road capability, and the engine and transmission had been modified to give greater acceleration and a higher top speed. Ros and the MI6 people then arrived and joined those already at the table and more introductions were made. The briefing then started at nine o'clock with Ros explaining that the Russian team was expected to arrive in the UK very soon. She hoped her Kremlin source would be able to give advance warning and the exact details of their arrival. If this didn't work she was confident she would be tipped off when they actually arrived or soon after.

She expected her source to inform her where Igor had decided to set up his base in the Westcountry. The worst case scenario would be that they would not immediately know where the Russians were staying. She explained that this would only be a temporary setback because once they knew the attackers were in the UK, it would not take long to trace them, because MI6 had full descriptions of Igor and Magd; the targets were known and Igor would have to have his base within striking distance of the targets.

Ros explained what Christine, William and Henry's roles were and the rules of engagement. It was not expected that firearms would be needed, but if armed conflict looked probable at any time she would request assistance from a police armed response unit or UK special forces. Last resort firearms would be carried by Gerald, Richard and Ox when and if necessary. Ros explained that the broad plan was to maintain surveillance and evidence-gathering contact with the Russians, remaining close enough to be able to summon armed assistance to arrest those involved just before they launched their attacks. After she finished she handed over to Gerald to explain how he expected his team to work the field.

Gerald had already mentioned most aspects of his briefing to Richard, Ox, Jackie and Andy, but he had never had them all together before. Now they were together, as well as the MI6 people they would be working with. He realised that seven plus himself and Maddie might seem like a lot of people. However, this number meant he would have various options to deal with the unexpected. They didn't know exactly how many Russian agents they would be up against or how or where they would work, and the more people they had on their side the more flexible they would be able to be. Because Gerald and Maddie might be recognised by Igor they would not get involved in any eyes-on surveillance.

Physical surveillance would be conducted by Richard and Ox, working separately or together, and the MI6 people. Transport would be provided by Jackie, and Gerald or Maddie would be the back-up drivers if required. Andy's job was electronic surveillance and evidence gathering.

Gerald re-emphasised that the key aim of the operation was to spring traps just before the attacks were mounted, arrest all the Russian agents, charge them and put them on public trial. This meant that Andy's role gathering visual and recorded evidence was crucial. His secondary role would be working with MI6 keeping electronic surveillance which would warn and guide Richard, Ox, Gerald and Maddie. Gerald and Maddie only had to avoid being seen by Igor and so could carry out surveillance of the others when Igor was not with them. That they had two VW campervans hadn't actually been planned but would clearly be an operational asset. William and Henry had a great range of surveillance equipment in their VW and would spend most of their time in the van. Old-fashioned bugs known as listening devices, a host of other radio, cell phone and remote line of sight laser listening devices gave them a huge array of surveillance options. The MI6 pair would maintain close contact with Handy Andy. Gerald expressed confidence that if they all worked well together as a team they would be able to deal with anything that might occur.

Gerald hoped they would get lucky and Ros would soon be informed where Igor and his team would be based. They would use the time until they found out where the Russians were getting to know each other, and driving to the North Cornwall coast at Bude to familiarise themselves with the area of operations.

Soon after breakfast a little convoy of vehicles left Tiverton Castle and took the A361 going west to Barnstaple, before joining the A39 to Bideford and on to Bude. The two VW campers followed Gerald and Maddie's Range Rover. The first VW was driven by Jackie whose passengers were Andy, Richard and Ox, and the second vehicle driven by Ros, had the MI6 team on board. The three vehicles were in touch using hand-held radios. Gerald acted as tour guide and while Maddie drove, he gave a running commentary on their route, places of interest and anything else he could think of that might be useful for everyone to know.

The first stop was the GCHQ site at Cleave Camp near the village of Morwenstow. Ros had called ahead and when the little convoy arrived the gates were opened and the vehicles swept through. Gerald, Richard and Ox particularly wanted to have a good look from the cliffs at the sea approaches. They were not approached by anyone in Cleave Camp and when they did pass close to people there were no good mornings or other greetings.

They drove around the camp, stopping frequently and using binoculars, checked out the countryside surrounding the area and making notes. Ros's source had reported that the attacks on the satellite dishes and the buildings would come from the sea; however, covering all bases had long been one of Gerald's golden rules, so he wanted to get a feel from where an attack might come if the Russian plan changed.

Forty-five minutes after the three vehicles had entered Cleave Camp the little convoy left. There happened to be two guards at the gate watching the vehicles leave, they waved but got no response.

"Friendly bastards, weren't they? Bloody spooks, probably Yanks, I reckon." The second guard was a dog handler and in response all he offered was, "Maybe," before strolling off to continue his patrol.

Half an hour later Gerald's group were parked at the car park on Crooklets Beach and everyone was in the Crooklets Beach Café for a light lunch. As they pulled into the car park Gerald and Ros had been conferring on the radio. They agreed that there would be no shop talk over lunch at the café.

After lunch the whole group walked the cliffs and beaches either side of Crooklets. They all knew that under Crooklets Beach was the transatlantic cable which was the second Russian target. Everywhere they walked they could see the Cleave Camp GCHQ satellite dishes perched on the cliffs approximately four miles north.

After the reconnaisance walkabout Gerald told everyone to spend the afternoon doing whatever they liked to familiarise themselves with Bude town and the immediate surrounding area, and then head back to Tiverton. He reckoned that all his people would learn and retain more if they did their own finding out rather than be taken on a further guided tour. At this stage Gerald had no idea what they would be up against. It could be a relatively simple matter of surveillance, observation and evidence gathering and making arrests, or it could turn into a much nastier game involving real danger. The more familiar his teams were with the ground on which they would be working the happier Gerald would be. He wanted his teams to effectively be on home ground as it would give them a considerable practical and tactical advantage over the Russians.

Back at the castle that night Gerald stuck to his no shop talk at dinner rule, but afterwards everyone remained at the table and talked about their day. It became obvious that a lot had been learned which could be invaluable. Gerald probed to find out where everyone had gone and what they had noted.

At one point it looked as if Richard, Ox, Jackie and Andy had spent a lot of time evaluating the merits of Bude's different pubs. Richard realised that Gerald was about to mention this and headed him off by reporting that Jackie had stuck to Coke Zeros, and they believed they had struck up good relations with the bar staff in a couple of places. These people would be happy to watch out for bad guys for them if asked.

Gerald nodded, smiled inwardly, and thought, Crafty old bugger, but didn't challenge Richard's logic as to the value of familiarity with local pub goers.

Ros reported that she had sent a message to her Moscow source asking for an update on the arrival of Igor's team. The answer that had come back was that there was a meeting the next morning which the source would be attending, and during which he hoped to find out the latest on the movements of Igor's team.

Gerald was happy to have more leeway before the opposition arrived. Time spent on preparation was never time wasted. He told everyone they would return to North Cornwall the next day. Richard and Ox would travel in the MI6 vehicle with Ros and Christine; William and Henry would go in Jackie's vehicle.

Gerald wanted them to go to Bude by the same route they had taken that day, but come back via Holsworthy and Okehampton on the A30 to Exeter and then on the A396 up the river Exe Valley to Bickleigh and Tiverton. Gerald couldn't turn them into locals within a few days, but the more familiar his people were with the potential area of operations the better. He had mixed the teams up because different pairs of eyes working together on these recces would notice different things and interpret them differently.

They were away all day and when they got back to Tiverton Ros had information which had come through to her while she was driving back from Bude. Igor and his people would arrive in London the following evening from Doha. Then the next day they would drive to Devon where coincidentally they also would be staying in a castle having booked three self-catering houses at the luxury Bovey Castle complex near Exeter.

Gerald was delighted, not only would they all soon be in action, but there was a clear day the next day before Igor would arrive, which gave them a chance to check out Bovey Castle and its surrounding area.

The other information from Ros was that Igor's men were all Syrians, and due to this Ros would be sending an Arabic speaker to join Gerald's team. Ros would have all incoming passenger lists from Doha flights checked and all the passengers would have photos taken by the cameras covering the arrival process. By the next night she expected to have all the data necessary to identify Igor and his whole team. Gerald and Ros were as ignorant as Igor and Magd had been that their arrival was also of interest to a pair of Kremlin killers.

Igor would not be arriving until the late afternoon; so Gerald and Maddie were able to go with the others to Bovey Castle the next day. They had booked lunch in two groups and also in two separate groups pretended interest in renting houses for family holidays.

Richard and Ox asked to be shown the three houses in Row C which are all together, and realised they had struck gold when the staff member showing them around mentioned that the three houses were being cleaned because they had all been taken from that evening. Richard immediately called Gerald after being shown around the houses, and Gerald called Handy Andy, William and Henry. A couple of hours later Handy Andy and the MI6 geeks feigned interest in renting one of the Row C lodges. They also were shown around all three houses and by the time they left all three contained electronic listening devices, and they also found places to hide tiny movement activated cameras which would cover the comings and goings of Igor's group.

They got back to Tiverton just before Fiona Edworthy was ready to dish up dinner. Gerald broke his no business at meal time rule because he wanted to debrief the Bovey Castle visit while it was still fresh in everyone's minds.

Ros announced that their Arabic speaker would be coming from London the next day so that they would get instant translations when Igor's group spoke Arabic among themselves.

William and Henry mentioned that when placing the cameras and listening devices they had been careful to position them in places where it would be all but impossible for them to be noticed unless a very thorough search was mounted. The cameras, for example, were not installed on the C lodges themselves but on the buildings opposite. Similarily the miniature microphones would be remotely activated and would not be turned on for twenty-four hours; so they would remain undetectable to allow Igor's team time to do a sweep to detect devices and come up with nothing.

Ros believed that it was almost certain that someone in Igor's team would have detection equipment and would be charged with making sure their lodges were free of devices. The concern wasn't just that the discovery of the devices would be an operational setback, it was also that if surveillance devices of any sort were detected it would tip Igor off and he would almost certainly abort his mission. Ensuring that neither Igor nor his people ever became aware of surveillance was vital to the success of the operation. For the trap to work it had to remain a trap, which it would cease to be if Igor realised his presence was known and he was being monitored.

Richard, Ox, Andy and Jackie would have to tail Igor, Magd or their men so unavoidably would be visible to them from time to time. However, William and Henry from the MI6 team would always work unseen; so Gerald and Ros decided that Christine, William, Henry and George, the recently arrived Arabic speaker, would go to dinner at Bovey Castle that night in case Igor's group decided to eat or drink in the bar or restauarant. If they did, then, using a range of covert miniature cameras, they would take photos of the Syrians, Igor and Magd. Christine and George would be seen later when conducting surveillance; so they both took the usual simple steps to alter their appearances as much as possible. If Arabic was spoken George would eavesdrop, and all four of the MI6 team would learn all they could by observation.

The other objective was that if Magd's team were all confirmed as being present in the bar or restaurant, Handy Andy would be tipped off and would attach tracker devices to the groups' three rental cars.

The driving distance from Bovey Castle to Tiverton is fifty-one miles. The MI6 team had dinner in Bovey Castle's main dining room and found themselves sitting at a table positioned between the two tables of four occupied by Igor's group. Richard, Ox, Andy and Jackie left the hotel as soon as Andy had attached his trackers. Their return drive took just over an hour, and an hour and a half later the MI6 group returned and everyone met in the dining room for a debrief.

Gerald and Ros were satisfied they had made a good start. They decided that because they were fifty miles away, which meant their reaction time was over an hour, they would stake out Bovey Castle from early the next morning. The advantage of the VW campers was that they looked like holiday vehicles so wouldn't attract attention, and the occupants of the vehicles could keep out of sight in the back. On the fringe of rural Dartmoor Range Rovers were a common sight, so Gerald's and Maddie's vehicle wouldn't attract attention. In his VW Jackie would take Richard, Ox and Andy to Bovey Castle the next day, park discreetly, and await developments. MI6 would park their VW campervan in a layby close to the end of the Bovey Castle entrance drive, near to where Gerald and Maddie would be in their Range Rover. The only person who would recognise Gerald and Maddie was Igor, so if Igor's group split and went in different directions Gerald and Maddie could follow any group of which Igor wasn't part.

The next morning they would leave for Bovey Castle at 05:45; so apart from William and Henry who headed for their VW campervan to check all their monitors, everyone was in bed asleep by 11:00. Gerald and Ros went to sleep both realising what a huge weight of responsibility rested on their shoulders. If the operation went as planned, they would deal a heavy blow to the Russians which would be significant to the West at a time of heightened global tension.

Soon after the MI6 team had finished dinner and left Bovey Castle Igor, Magd and the others left their table and went to the hotel bar for a drink before heading back to their lodges.

They spoke Arabic and English and switched from one language to the other reverting to Arabic when they were talking about things they didn't want nearby listeners to understand. While Igor was in overall charge Magd was the operational chief of his fellow Syrians. He decided that the next day the diving team would go to the local diving equipment shops they had researched and start looking for the kit they would need. The anglers would drive to Brixham where they would arrange a couple of days' sea fishing on an angling charter boat.

Igor decided that he and Magd would drive over to Bude to get familiar with the area and look for a boat they could charter for their initial sea reconnaisance.

Igor hadn't shaved since he landed at Heathrow Airport and was trying to use an American accent when he spoke English. It was a very long shot that he might run into Gerald, Maddie, the angling skipper, or anyone else he had met on his weekend in Bude all those years ago. However, as a Russian he would stand out which would increase the chance of him being remembered. He hoped that with a beard, with his once dark hair now having gone grey and his American accent the already slim chance of his being recognised would be close to zero.

They all walked back to their lodges and didn't realise that there were various pieces of electronic equipment hearing and seeing much of their activity.

At Tiverton Castle William and Henry were in the VW van working with colleagues at GCHQ in Cheltenham and at the MI6 communications centre setting up ways of monitoring as much of the Syrian's communications as possible. Igor had not allowed any of Magd's group to bring their computers, cell phones or other electronic devices. This was working in his favour because apart from Magd's cellphone he had the only internet equipment which meant that Henry and William were drawing a blank intercepting communications and were relying on their cameras and listening devices.

The pair were just about to call it a night when Henry who was wearing headphones handed a second set to William and said, "Hmmm, interesting, have a listen."

They listened together to the unmistakable sounds of a couple having sex in the lodge occupied by Igor and Magd. There was only one camera in the lodge which covered the lounge area which was dark and had no one in it. They were listening to a bug in Magd's bedroom and until there was a cry which came from a female, they thought the couple must have been Igor and Magd.

There was no way they could have known that Magd was watching a pornography channel on his cellphone in his bedroom, and the actors were a very young white girl and a middle-aged black man. They could also not have known that Magd's sexual appetites would soon play a part in the story that was starting to unfold.

Over two hundred miles to the east of Bovey and Tiverton Castles Yevgeny and Alexei were having dinner at the Mari Vanna Russian Restaurant in Knightsbridge. They weren't hurrying their dinner but were looking forward to getting back to their hotel where they had arranged to be visited by two call girls. Several hundred miles to the north the crew of an ocean-going Irish fishing boat were going about their business. Within a short time the Russian killers and the Irish fishing boat would both converge on the North Cornwall area to play their parts in the drama which was starting to unfold.

PART TWO

The Game Takes Shape

10

At 05:45 the next morning at five minute intervals the two Range Rovers and the MI6 VW campervan left Tiverton Castle on the A396 heading for Exeter. After Exeter the three vehicles then went a short distance along the A30 before turning off onto the B3212 for Moretonhampstead and Bovey Castle.

There was almost no traffic; so all Gerald's players were in place just after 07:00. The trackers which Handy Andy had placed under each of Igor's three vehicles meant that as soon as those vehicles moved Gerald's teams would know about it.

Due to this Gerald and Maddie in their Range Rover; Ox, Richard and Andy in Jackie's Range Rover, and the MI6 team in the VW were all able to park in places that wouldn't attract attention, safe in the knowledge that to tail their targets no one needed visual contact after the Arab vehicles had left Bovey Castle. Gerald wanted each of the three target vehicles to be followed; the tracking devices would enable Andy to direct each team in pursuit of an opposition car without needing to see it as it came out of the main gate. Anticipating that the opposition would split into three teams Gerald had named them Russia One, Arab One and Arab Two.

It was a long wait but just after 09:00 the first hire car came through the castle gate, and hadn't gone a mile before the MI6 VW was on its tail. Handy Andy had worked with William and Henry and they also connected the tracker devices into the systems in their VW. The MI6 team were tailing Daoud,

Suleiman and Ahmed who were the anglers, and who joined the A382 towards Bovey Tracey before making their way towards the Torbay coast and Brixham.

A couple of minutes after the anglers had left Bovey Castle, Igor and Magd drove out through the same gate. Andy sat beside Jackie in the Range Rover and watched the screen on a laptop which was receiving the signal from the tracker in Russia One which was Igor's vehicle. Igor had limited options and Jackie guessed he would head towards Moretonhampstead. He decided to get ahead of him and wait. He was right, and they only had a couple of minutes to wait before Igor and Magd drove by and turned onto the A382 heading for where it joined the A30.

Andy called Gerald on his burner cell phone. "Hi Boss, if I had to make a guess I would say Russia One is going to Bude. He will hit the A30 in a couple of minutes and I reckon he'll head towards Okehampton, then Bude." Andy's screen was divided into four squares, one was blank and the others showed the positions of the three vehicles they were tracking.

Gerald was about to acknowledge Andy's comment when he continued, "Get ready, Boss, Arab Two is now on the move, you should see him any minute."

There was a slight pause before Gerald answered. "Roger, he has just passed us, we're on him now." Gerald's team now kept in regular contact with Andy and it soon became clear that Russia One almost certainly was heading for Bude. Arab One and Two were important, but Igor was Gerald's prime concern that day, so he called the team tailing them. "I want eyes on Igor and Magd all the time. If it is Bude, and it almost certainly is, then use every trick in the book to keep close tabs on them but make sure they don't spot your surveillance. If they split up once they are there, then you guys split up and make sure you don't lose either of them. All the normal stuff, work singly, work in pairs and chop and change all the time. There shouldn't be any need to talk now unless something urgent comes up, and if it does, call Maddie. Notice everything and note everything. At the end of the day escort our friends safely back to Bovey; then head for Tiverton. We'll do a full round table briefing this evening."

Gerald called Christine, William, Henry and George in the MI6 VW and gave them a similar message. Christine had her cell on speakerphone, so everyone heard Gerald's instructions. Christine responded with, "Understood," and George's contribution was, "Ripping."

Ross had taken the train back to London that morning, leaving Christine in charge of the MI6 group. The two techies, Henry and William, were wholly absorbed in keeping in touch with Andy and using their own hi-tech kit. They didn't care who their boss was, and George had happily fallen in under Christine's command because she was older, had field experience and worked directly under Ros.

George was a product of the public school system, had two first-class degrees from Oxford relating to the Middle East, was a fluent Arabist and seemed to regard life as one big adventure populated by the forces of darkness and light. When speaking English his conversation was peppered with words and phrases like "spiffing", "ripping" and "tip top, old bean".

Richard and Ox found his expressions highly amusing thinking that such words had stopped being used decades ago, but George's manner of speaking irritated Handy Andy and Jackie Stewart and Andy quickly dubbed George, "Mohammed Fauntleroy". The description was lost on Jackie who still seemed confused even after Andy had explained it to him!

When Ros had called her MI6 group together and emphasised that Christine was in charge, George had commented, "Roger that, Ros, whizzo, what fun!"

Christine's eyes rolled back in her head and Andy simply glared. However, by the end of what had now been given the name "Operation Ahead of the Game", everyone would have a high opinion of the Arabic speaker with the posh English Bertie Wooster public school accent.

Andy's guess proved correct: Igor and Magd did drive to Bude and then to Morwenstow, and pretty much duplicated the recce which Gerald's team had done earlier. Arab One, the anglers, went to Brixham where they chartered a boat for two days' sea fishing. On the advice of the skipper the charter would start two days later after a weather front had gone through. After booking the charter, Daoud, Ahmed and Suleiman went to a tackle shop to buy rods, reels and all the other kit they would need to make them look like experienced anglers.

Arab Two, Mohammed, Khalifa and Akram formed the diving group and they went first to Exeter, then to Teignmouth, before heading for Plymouth, shopping for their underwater kit.

Gerald and his two teams successfully tailed their targets all day, and once each team had followed them back to Bovey Castle they headed for Tiverton and the evening debrief.

The MI6 vehicle was fitted with a range of electronic devices which were constantly fussed over by William and Henry who hadn't left the rear of their VW van all day. The physical "eyes on" surveillance of Arab One, the anglers, had been carried out by Christine and George.

During the day the MI6 VW had naturally evolved as the command vehicle and Handy Andy fed everything he picked up to William and Henry, as did Gerald and Maddie by calling in regularly.

Fiona and Tom Edworthy had a buffet supper waiting for everyone on their return to Tiverton, and Fiona was delighted that all the food disappeared. No one had lunch and so everyone was hungry. Fiona who almost had the appearance of a school matron making sure that all her children ate up, was watching them while they ate! On one occasion in the conversation George did refer to Fiona as "the matron", but it didn't happen again because "the matron" asked him whether he would like a clip round the ear.

This had been the first action day and the after dinner de-briefs were eagerly awaited by everyone.

While Gerald and his group were tailing their subjects in Devon, about 190 miles to the East of Tiverton Castle in London's Notting Hill, Yevgeny and Alexei were having a drink in their hotel bar. They wanted to leave as few trails as possible so had not hired a car to take them to the Westcountry.

Instead they had found a second-hand car dealer and hand-ed over £12,500 in cash for a 2016 4 Series BMW. Earlier in the day the car dealer had received a phone call not only asking him what cars he had for sale at around £10,000-12,000, but also ask-ing if he was the owner of the business and enquiring whether he could arrange insurance if they bought a car. At the time he wondered why the caller needed to know whether he was talk-ing to the dealership owner and why he couldn't arrange his own insurance. However, because the caller was obviously for-eign he shrugged if off and left it at that.

When Yevgeny counted out £12,500 in £20 notes the car dealer realised something dodgy might be happening, but it didn't stop him accepting the cash and making out a receipt as requested to Mr A. Karloff. Yevgeny took the receipt, winked, then said, "Good to do business, my friend." He then winked again, picked up the keys and a print-out of the insurance cover and handed over another £500 saying, "Just a little present, my friend," and walked out of the office, followed by Alexei.

While the dealer was very pleased with the sale because it had been cash he realised he now had to find a way of making the 4 Series BMW disappear from his stock list. Without thinking he had told Yevgeny he would register the car with the authorities, and now he wondered how the hell he was going to do it. He had the new owner's details due to having arranged the insurance, but was now fairly sure all that information was false. Still he was happy with the risk. £13,000 was £13,000 it was in cash, the profit margin was good and the tax man wouldn't see any of it.

11

At Tiverton Castle everyone sat with coffee or a glass of wine and listened while Richard and Ox reported what happened through the day as they followed Russia One, Igor and Magd, who did take the route Andy had predicted. They had gone straight to the Crooklets Beach area. It was low tide and they had walked onto the beach before heading north up the expanse of sand towards Northcott Mouth about one and a half miles away.

Ox followed them along the beach and Richard walked the cliffs above the beach, keeping them all in sight. Igor and Magd took several photos as they walked, both of the beach and, once they were in view, the GCHQ dishes on the clifftop ahead of them. They left the beach at Northcott and walked back along the cliffs to Bude.

Once they were on the cliff path Richard followed them and Ox walked back along the beach towards Crooklets. While on the cliffs Igor and Magd had often stopped and looked back towards the GCHQ dishes and taken more photographs. After getting back to Crooklets the Russian and the Syrian sat outside the Crooklets Beach Café drinking coffee, while Richard, Ox, Andy and Jackie watched them from Rosie's Café on the other side of the small river.

After finishing their coffee the Russian and the Syrian went back to their vehicle and drove north out of Bude up the A39 before turning left just before Kilkhampton onto a by-road leading towards Stibb, Coombe Valley and Morwenstow. In the narrow winding lanes the tracker under Russia One made it possible for them to tail Igor at a distance and avoid detection. When Richard was relating this and explained this point, George was heard to mutter, "Spiffing, good work," which drew a smile from Ox, the usual scowl from Andy and raised eyebrows from Christine.

Igor and Magd had done a thorough reconnaisance job of the whole area around the GCHQ site, checking out all the approach routes and often stopping for a minute or two. Richard explained that although they had a track of the route covered by Russia One they did not have eyes on when Igor's vehicle had stopped, so couldn't be sure why he had done so.

After Igor had left the GCHQ area he drove to the A39 and when he reached Stratton turned left, taking the road towards Holsworthy. Jackie had parked his Range Rover in Stratton and they had all watched Andy's screen which showed where Igor was going. Richard had suggested it was safe to assume that Russia One was heading back to Bovey, and had rung Gerald to get permission to give up the tail and return to the GCHQ area to check out the places where Igor had stopped.

Richard reported that all three of the places where Igor had stopped had been on high ground with good views of the dishes at GCHQ. He thought that although Ros's information was that GCHQ would be attacked from the sea, maybe Igor was checking to see if an attack from the inland side might also be possible.

After Richard had finished, Gerald reported on Arab Two. Khalifa, Akram and Mohammed had driven to Teignmouth to a shop called Teign Diving Centre, and then to another diving shop in Plymouth called Aquanauts. Between the two shops they had spent a considerable amount of money on masks, snorkels, wetsuits, dry suits, BCD jackets, diving knives, cylinders and other equipment.

Maddie had followed them into one shop and Gerald into

the other. They were not especially interested in which kit had been bought, they were more interested in assessing their targets and learning about their behaviour: How many cell phones they had, did they speak good English, were they armed in any way, and who was the leader of the group. Each time they got back to their vehicle Gerald and Maddie made written notes of everything they could remember. They believed firmly that the more one knows about one's enemy, the better.

They had watched them in the dive shops, while having lunch in a pub and while walking around exploring both Teignmouth and Plymouth. By listening to the conversations in the shops it was obvious that two of the Syrians in particular were expert divers. The third, who would later be identified as Akram, did not take part in the equipment buying discussions in the shops, but his eyes did follow most of the attractive girls they came across during the day.

Their pub visit at lunchtime had yielded the information that none of the three were particularly strict Muslims. They each drank a couple of beers, and didn't seem worried about what they ate. By the end of the day Gerald and Maddie were confident their surveillance had not been noted, and they had learnt a lot which might prove useful later on in the game.

Christine was the last to report. She and George had stuck close to the anglers all day and George had tried to be within listening distance as much as possible. She made a point of commending George on his work saying that he was one of the slipperiest shadows she had ever seen operating. George looked pleased at this comment and Andy looked rather surprised at the compliment.

The Brixham Bait and Tackle shop owner thought that Christmas and his birthday had all come at once when the three Syrians walked in and spent over £3,000 on fishing rods, reels, clothing and other equipment. The owner quickly put the card machine away when he saw Daoud produce his large wad of £20 notes. The tackle shop recommended a local angling charter skipper and gave his mobile number to the angling group. Like the diving group the anglers spent lunchtime in a pub and then went in search of the angling skipper to book their fishing charter. Also like the diving group the anglers seemed unconcerned about what they ate and were very happy drinking alcohol.

After they had all reported Gerald gave George the job of building profiles on all eight members of their opposition. George and Christine then spent time together listing everything they could remember about the anglers, and George quizzed Richard's group and Gerald and Maddie for everything they could remember about their targets, before going back to Christine to work on the profiles.

The same debriefing exercise was happening in reverse at Bovey Castle, where in Igor's lodge, with loud Arabic music being played, the anglers and divers reported in detail everything they had done.

In Moscow Magd had listed the weapon systems and explosives which he wanted to be on the Irish vessel: RPGs, shoulder-fired missiles, various types of drones and explosives and an assortment of rifles, machine guns and handguns that would give him choices once he had assessed the targets and made his decisions. He had also given his employers the names of three shady Arab arms dealers in case the Russians thought that buying weapons from these people would help further muddle the trail and lend credibility to the presence of the IPF in the game. He explained to his men that although more sea recces still needed to be done he was starting to think that First

Person View or FPV drones should be used for the attack on the GCHQ installations. The drones could be flown in from a small vessel sitting a short distance offshore and would then approach low and fast to reduce any possibility of detection and interception by rockets or missiles. However, while FPV drones were one option, the others were preprogrammed drones to reduce any chance of radio jamming, or rockets or missiles. Magd made clear that speed would be essential both in terms of the attack itself and the escape afterwards.

After the debriefing the diving and angling teams went back to their respective lodges without knowing that Andy's cameras outside Igor's lodge had recorded both their arrivals and their departures.

George and Andy had listened in ever increasing frustration to the loud Arabic music being played while Igor debriefed his people. After the meeting, when Igor made a report to Moscow, neither Andy nor the MI6 techies picked it up. When Igor was reporting to his FSB control Magd walked back to the hotel where he had earlier noticed a young woman serving behind the bar who seemed very friendly. She was very much his type although at twenty years old was a couple of years older than the really young women he preferred.

Magd was the only customer in the bar and they spent half an hour laughing and chatting. He passed £200 across the bar in cash and told the girl that he wanted her to buy herself something special. She first tried to refuse the gift, she then put it in a pocket of her skirt saying that she didn't know how to thank him. Magd could think of several ways she could thank him but said nothing; he would give her an opportunity to thank him in the next day or so. He finished his drink watching her in her white blouse and short tight black skirt as she packed up the bar. While observing her body move he conjured up images of what was hidden under her clothes. Magd might appear charming with a capital C, but his sexual appetites could be cruel, also with a capital C.

June Symonds watched Magd leave and repeated the cheery good night she had already wished him, and then for good measure added, "Sleep tight." When Magd turned and waved she gave him a dazzling smile. She would have behaved very differently had she known what lay ahead.

Igor's decades of working in the secret world had produced various rules which he used to guide his actions. Among these were: never step out of character, keep things simple and, when appropriate, hiding in plain sight was often an effective tool of the trade.

For his reports to the FSB he used the "keep it simple" rule. He typed his messages privately and ahead of time on an encrypted device and then used Virtual Private Networks (VPNs) to send his messages to Moscow. He planned to change networks regularly, and most of the time would send his messages from public places such as cafés and restaurants with a lack of CCTV, and where he would only spend a limited period of time.

By employing these basic tactics and varying the days, times and locations of his communications, Igor was essentially a "ghost" online and his reports were unlikely to be flagged as "of interest" to anyone. As an extra layer of security both he and Moscow used word codes and offline programmes which translated their messages alternately into French and German.

12

Gerald's and the other two vehicles were back at Bovey Castle early the next morning, standing by to follow Russia One, Arab One and Arab Two. To avoid being recognised Gerald and Maddie could not follow Igor, but they did switch from the Arab Two team which they had followed the day before to Arab One. Richard's team followed Arab Two and the MI6 VW tailed Igor and Magd.

Arab One went to Exmouth where they went reef fishing in the morning and mackerel fishing in the afternoon. Gerald and Maddie did not go with them on either trip because Gerald was confident the Syrians were doing nothing more than fishing, and being in close proximity to their targets for prolonged periods would ensure they were recognised in the future which had to be avoided.

Gerald was right; the fishing trips were innocent. All the Syrian anglers were doing was familiarising themselves with local fishing jargon and practices.

Richard's team followed Arab Two to Cornwall where they spent two hours at a boatyard called Rock Marine near Wadebridge. After the Syrians had left Richard and Ox went into the Rock Marine office to see what they could find out. When they expressed interest in buying a boat the salesman let slip that he had already sold a boat that day only about an hour ago.

Christine and the MI6 team followed Igor and Magd to Bude and then Christine and George took turns to keep them under surveillance. They alternated frequently to reduce the chance of the Russian and the Syrian spotting they had a tail.

Once again Gerald held a debrief after dinner. Igor's people were clearly moving fast, putting into action plans which had been made before their arrival in Britain. Ros's Moscow source was now of less value; so keeping close surveillance on all of Igor's people was vital.

In the past Gerald and Ros had had warning from Moscow as to what was going to happen, which meant they could be proactive to a degree. Now that Igor was making his decisions locally the game had changed and they were having to be reactive to what they saw and heard on the ground.

Gerald and Maddie didn't take long describing what the anglers had done. Interest increased when Richard reported that it looked likely that the Arab Two team had bought a boat from the yard near Wadebridge.

Last to report was Christine. She and George had parked near the Falcon Hotel in Bude and alternately had followed Igor and Magd along the side of the canal basin to where they had met a man near the lockgates. The meeting had obviously been pre-arranged and the MI6 techies and Andy were all disappointed that they hadn't picked this up beforehand. This underlined that they didn't have a full-time reliable way of monitoring all the calls being made by the opposition.

Christine had noticed Magd looking at her; so when it came to getting close to Igor, Magd and the man they were talking to, she called George who made the approach, and was able to stand close enough to pick up much of what was said while pretending to take photographs.

Christine suspected that Magd had only been looking at

The Falcon Hotel on the canal in Bude where Richard, Ox, Igor and Magd all stayed.

her intently because she was a woman, but she got out of his sight quickly, hoping he wouldn't remember her. She had been wearing sunglasses, a bright red jacket and had her hair in a ponytail. She made a mental note to ensure that the sunglasses, ponytail and red coat were not part of her appearance when next she saw Magd.

By pretending interest in photographing various features George had managed to stay close to Igor and Magd as they chatted to what looked like a local fisherman. He had heard much of what was said and was fairly sure they were arranging a fishing trip for two days later. George was right, the man they had been talking to was Vincent Headon, the Bude harbour master, who had a boat called *Mantra* and who did fishing charters.

When around Bovey Castle there was now no reason for Igor's party to appear to not know each other. They were all staying in lodges close to each other, seven out of eight of them were Arabs, and although they had checked in separately they had made a point of meeting in the bar of the hotel on both of the previous evenings.

The hotel had arranged a table for eight in the dining room and they discussed their day in a mixture of English and Arabic. Igor was pleased with progress and at the end of dinner he summed up the actions that would be taken over the next seven days.

In two day's time he and Magd would return to Bude for their fishing trip which would actually be a reconnaisance of GCHQ from the sea. The anglers would go to sea for the first of their two fishing days, and the diving group would return to Rock Marine to take delivery of the boat and put her in the water in a short-term berth they had agreed to rent from Rock Marine for two weeks.

Before the attacks the anglers and divers would both familiarise themselves with the 6.5 metre Leeward 18 boat which had been bought for £25,000. Igor gave Akram a visa card with a £30,000 credit limit which he told him he should use to pay for the boat. The divers would use the boat for their dive when they would place the explosive charges on the Google cable, and the anglers would charter Vincent's boat for the day of the attack on GCHQ from the sea. Igor and Magd would remain on shore that day so there would only be four people on Vincent's boat.

Four people would put to sea but only three would later head fast offshore making their escape.

Once Magd's Syrians were confident in their boat and their boat handling, weather permitting, they would go to sea and rendezvous with the Irish trawler for the transfer of the weapons and equipment to be used in the attacks.

Apart from June Symmonds there were only three other people in the bar. They were all men, all foreign and she thought they were German.

After dinner Igor, the divers and anglers had walked in a group from the hotel back to their lodges, but Magd had headed for the bar. June brightened visibly when he walked in. She asked him what he wanted and giggled when he said that what he wanted was a naughty girl. She had Magd's £200 in her bedside table at home and had spent much of the day deciding whether to spend it in Plymouth or Exeter, and what to spend it on.

He ordered a Glenlivet malt whisky and asked her what

she would like. She giggled again and said she wasn't allowed to drink in the bar but liked lots of different things. She was flirting and Magd caught the double meaning in her reply. He smiled, slid a £20 note over the bar and told her to keep the change. The change went quickly into the same pocket in her skirt which had held the £200 the night before.

It was 10:30 when the three Germans left the bar heading for their rooms. Magd asked her what time she finished work. She told him she could shut the bar and pack up at 11:00 if there were no customers. For the next fifteen minutes Magd gently and skillfully flattered June who took all the compliments to heart and was clearly very impressed by the rich, good-looking, smooth Arab.

Just before 11:00 Magd invited her to come back to his lodge for a quick drink on her way home. With stars and cash in her eyes and head she accepted.

She lived in Moretonhampstead and every day drove the two and a half miles to work in the hotel. The hotel was not full and it was late, so she decided she would risk parking her car close to Magd's lodge. Staff parking was only allowed in the staff car park, and if she were caught visiting a guest in a room or lodge she would be fired. When accepting Magd's invitation and deciding to park her car close to his lodge her mind hadn't been on the risks, she was absorbed by the lure of adventure and possible romance and gifts.

Magd walked back to his lodge and was happy to note that Igor was in his room and his lights were off. He left the front door open and went to his room to take a shower and wait.

As Magd was walking back to his lodge a 4 series BMW with two men inside was driving up the Bovey Castle main drive towards the hotel. Frankie Pinter was at the hotel's front desk and was aware of the headlights outside when she smiled at June and said goodnight to the bar girl as she left. Minutes later Yevgeny and Alexei, each carrying a light case walked in through the hotel's front door and approached Frankie to check in.

13

June was both excited and nervous as she walked from her car to Magd's lodge in Row C. Igor was asleep as were the three Syrian divers, and the angling group were watching the CIA saving the world from bad guys on a video. Magd had showered and was sitting waiting for June dressed in a long Arab dishdasha-style garment. She pushed at the open front door and stepped in apprehensively.

Magd said, "Hello, I am so happy you came." He got up, crossed to the door and shut it behind the nervous twenty year-old. "Would you like a drink of whisky, or maybe some wine?"

June's heart was in her mouth as she answered, "Wine, please."

Magd handed June his whisky glass together with a wine glass, took a bottle of white wine from the fridge, and carrying the wine and whisky bottles headed for the stairs. "Come with me, let's go upstairs for a drink."

There were two armchairs in the bedroom and they each sat in one with their drinks. Magd was friendly and charming and June started to lose her nervousness and relax. He asked her lots of questions about herself and her family and seemed genuinely interested in her life. Every now and then either one of them would glance at the American comedy movie playing on the TV with the sound turned low.

What had been a full bottle of Chardonnay was over half empty when June said she needed to go to the bathroom. She had a pee, touched up her lipstick and squirted a little perfume on her neck. She expected sex would happen. She had never been with a foreign man before and the idea excited her.

When she came back into the room Magd smiled and pulled his long robe over his head and as the garment rose up his legs and past his middle June saw he was naked and his penis was fully erect.

When the robe had cleared his head he bundled it up and threw it on a chair while smiling and crossing the room to June. Still smiling he took her hand and put it on his penis then he started to undress her. There was a large cell phone on its side on a stand on the dresser behind him. While he took off her clothes she stared mesmerised at the small screen on which a pornographic film was playing.

She hadn't really noticed yet but there was no kissing and no tenderness. Once she was naked he stroked her body but it was a firm, almost rough caress. They were standing face to face when he stooped down and ran his hand up the inside of her thighs, separating them. When he got to the top of her legs he thrust a finger deep into her vagina and she gasped in protest. He withdrew his finger, smiled and said, "Nice and tight."

June had stopped rubbing his penis and now stood like a statue as Magd pushed a hand into the cleft between her buttocks. He moved to a bedside table and picked up a small glass bottle from which he sniffed deeply at as he carried it to June.

June's earlier excitement hadn't yet turned into real fear and she was wary of upsetting the powerful male figure in front of her, so she did so, too.

Magd put the bottle down and said, "Get on the bed."

This was not romantic and wasn't what June had expected; the white wine and amyl nitrate had charged her senses but not enough to stop her feeling that there was now an air of menace in the room.

She got on the bed and lay waiting for him, while he put

some sort of grease or oil on his penis. He came to the bed and roughly turned her over onto her stomach. She turned her head and started to scream, "No!" as she felt fingers probing for her anus and received a heavy stinging slap.

Magd lifted her buttocks and entered her from behind while holding one hand over her mouth to stop her screaming. It was a brutal assault and her shoulders, lower back, buttocks and the back of her legs would all soon show livid bruising.

When Magd had finished she squirmed off the bed and sobbing went to put her clothes on. She was grabbed from behind and slapped again before being flung back on the bed.

June was a country girl, had grown up with three brothers and had learned how to fight. When Magd came to her on the bed she slapped him and tried to knee him in the groin. This resistance prompted two more hard blows from the Syrian. The second split her lip and knocked her almost unconscious.

When she was again fully alert she realised that Magd had used his belt and secured her hands together to the headboard above her head. June was too frightened to think clearly as she watched him have another gulp of whisky followed by another deep sniff of amyl nitrate. He played with his penis applying more oil and smiled without taking his eyes off her as she lay on the bed. When he got on top and tried to enter her she kept her thighs tightly together. This earned her another slap but this time Magd did not have his hand over her mouth, so her scream was not silenced.

Igor did not know what had wakened him but seconds after what he thought was a scream he heard signs of a struggle in Magd's room. He went upstairs and opened the door to Magd's room to see his naked buttocks rise and fall as he thrust into a young woman struggling and writhing on the bed which had several bloodstains on it.

Magd became aware of Igor in the door and hissed, "Isla barra, get out!" Igor could only think of their operation and how something like this could wreck it. Very firmly and calmly, he looked at Magd and ordered, "Stop and get her out of here, now."

Magd was unable to climax. He rolled off June and suddenly the combined effect of sex, whisky, adrenalin and amyl nitrate hit him. He got off the bed and sat in a chair watching June crying on the bed and struggling to free her hands. He was about to release her when she freed herself, darted to her clothes and started dressing.

The door opened and again Igor was there with the same command: "Get her out of here."

June dressed fast and as best as she could. She knew she had blood on her face, between her legs and on her back. She didn't care about cleaning herself, she just wanted to leave as quickly as possible. She was picking up her car keys and bag from the dresser when Magd handed her a fistful of £20 notes and said, "Take this and keep quiet. Say anything to anyone and I will tell them you are a whore."

June spat in Magd's face, slapped his hand, scattering the money to the floor and stumbled out of the house sobbing as she ran to her car.

Magd cleaned himself up in the bathroom, put his dishdasha back on and walked back into the bedroom to find Igor sitting in a chair waiting for him. The Russian was clearly very angry.

"You are an idiot, why couldn't you keep it in your pants until we finished our job? If that girl goes to the police our whole operation will be finished. I will think about it but maybe we will have to leave here in a few hours. Get some sleep."

Igor had nothing more to say so he got up and left the room.

He closed the door but didn't notice that it hadn't latched and had swung open about an inch.

Magd didn't say anything; he just shrugged at Igor's departing back, then got onto the bed and was asleep in minutes.

June lived on the Bovey Castle side of Morehampstead. It normally took her about twelve minutes to drive home from work. That night, driving in a daze of alcohol, pain and a mixture of fear and relief the short drive took twice as long. It was 1:40 am when she parked outside her parents' house and crept in as quietly as she could through the back door which opened into the kitchen. She was almost thinking straight now, and while she didn't know what she was going to do about the assault, she did know that she didn't want her parents and brothers involved until she had come to terms with what had happened and worked it out.

Reuben was the eldest of June's three brothers and the only one not to be named after the American rock band *Guns n' Roses*. Reuben's parents were huge fans of the band and Reuben's brothers, Axl and Steven, were named after the singer and the drummer. The band's great hit "Sweet Child o' Mine" could often be heard blaring out from the Symonds's family home. June was the youngest of the four siblings, and although her brothers had grown up treating her like a boy they were also fiercely protective of her.

Reuben, Axl and Steven were all large men and all three worked on building sites. Reuben was a keen rugby player. Years ago he had had a trial for the Exeter Chiefs which resulted in him training twice a week and playing regularly for the second fifteen while dreaming of promotion and first fifteen glory. He no longer played rugby but weekly visits to the gym and

110

working on building sites kept his 6 ft 4 in body very fit and in good shape. His brother Axl had come in late, just after 1:00 am which had woken Reuben up. He went to the bathroom for a pee and when he came back he noticed his sister's car wasn't there which was unusual because when working the evening shift June was usually home from work at about 11:45 pm.

Reuben tried to go back to sleep but his little sister's absence played on his mind and kept him awake. He was still awake at 1:40 am when June's headlights briefly flooded his room. He heard the engine approach, then die as she turned it off. Why he got out of bed and went downstairs he would never know, but he was standing in the kitchen doorway when June came in from outside.

She didn't turn the light on but she didn't need to for Reuben to see her distress and the blood on her face from her split lip. He said, "Hello sister," shut the door very quietly behind her and turned the light on.

June said nothing in reply, she burst into tears, took three steps and flung her arms around her big brother. Devonians are no different from other Britons in that cups of tea often come to the rescue in difficult situations. Reuben held his sister for a minute as her sobbing slowly subsided. He then gently pushed her away to arms' length and said, "Go and get washed up. I'll put the kettle on for a cup of tea and you come back and tell me all about it."

June and her brothers were not shy towards each other. She had often seen them naked when growing up and thought little of it. June undressed and flannel washed herself in the bathroom before going downstairs in her dressing gown. She was very clear headed and very detailed when she told her story to her elder brother.

When she had finished Reuben asked if she was wearing anything under her dressing gown, she replied that she had underwear on.

"Do you mind taking that gown off, sister, I want to see what he did to you."

June stood before her brother in knickers and bra while he circled her noting bruising in many places on her body as well as her split lip and one very swollen eye above a badly bruised cheek. He didn't say a word while he examined her, he then helped her back into her dressing gown, kissed her on the forehead and told her to go and get some sleep.

Half an hour later June was sinking into a troubled sleep while in the next room Reuben shook his brother Axl's shoulder to wake him. "Come on, Axl, wake up, mate, we have some work to do. Meet me downstairs."

Ten minutes later, bent on revenge, June's two big brothers were driving towards Bovey Castle.

"We'll toast this bastard, I'll make the fucker wish he had never even bloody seen our sister."

June had told Reuben which lodge Magd was staying in and which bedroom he occupied. The Symonds family were very familiar with Bovey Castle. At one time or another June's parents and her brothers had worked there in various capacities.

Reuben knew exactly which lodge June had referred to. He had only one objective in mind, and although he wasn't in a blind rage little details like how they would get into Magd's lodge hadn't yet concerned him. The brothers were totally confident that they could handle Magd and give him a lesson he would remember. They didn't know that Magd was a trained killer, and had a team around him made up of men for whom violence was part of life.

Reuben parked in the car park closest to Magd's lodge in Row C. They approached the house stealthily without realising that they were being watched by Handy Andy's cameras. The front door which Magd had earlier left open for June had now been locked for the night by Igor. After trying the front door the brothers checked all the ground floor windows and found one which Axl opened and got through.

A minute later the pair was going up the stairs, heading for the room which June had told Reuben was occupied by Magd. Andy's cameras had not picked up Axl going through the window, but he was filmed opening the front door and his and Reuben's progress through the house and up the stairs was also recorded on his audio listening device.

When Igor had left Magd's bedroom earlier, the door latch hadn't quite caught; so now when Reuben pushed gently against the handle the door opened silently. The brothers overpowered Magd quickly and a minute and a half later he was lying naked on the floor with a small hand towel stuffed into his mouth and with his hands and feet tied together. An irony which the brothers weren't aware of, and Magd didn't register, was that the same belt which earlier had secured June's wrists, was now around Magd's ankles.

When driving to Bovey Castle Reuben could only think of punching and kicking the man who had assaulted his little sister. He was now getting much more satisfaction watching Magd's terrified eyes fixed on the knife he was holding very close to his penis and testicles.

Axl watched both of them and kept his ears open for any

noise which might indicate that their presence in the house had been discovered. Reuben lifted Magd's testicles with the flat of his blade and then used it to stroke Magd's penis which shrivelled, retreating rapidly. He bent down and whispered in Magd's ear, "Not much fun, is it, mate, when someone can play with your dick and cut it off?"

Reuben's jacket hung over the back of a chair and he fetched a small heavy-looking hammer from a side pocket. In the bathroom he found a second small hand towel like the one he had earlier thrust into Magd's mouth. He picked up Magd's left hand and placed it palm down on the towel he had folded and placed on the floor. With his knee on Magd's wrists Reuben swung the small hammer and smashed Magd's left hand index finger. The towel under Magd's hands had dulled the noise of the blow to a thud when the hammer hit the finger on the carpet, then there was a second muffled thud as he hit it again. Magd convulsed in shock and pain but with Axl kneeling on his chest and thighs and Reuben securing his wrists he could only writhe in agony.

"Now for the other one; good fun this, matey, isn't it? Now then, eenie meenie miney moe, which one shall we manicure next? Miney, that'll do!"

There was another crunching thud as Magd's right hand ring finger was smashed. He was now sweating profusely as he writhed and a grunting moaning noise came from behind the towel in his mouth.

"Mustn't forget my sister's face, me old pal."

Next the hammer's wooden handle was used to attack Magd's face, splitting his upper lip, opening up a gash on one of his cheekbones and causing several red blotches which would soon become livid bruises where the hammer handle had struck.

Reuben's anger had gone as he watched Magd lying bruised and broken on the floor.

"C'mon, brother, let's go 'ome."

Without realising it Reuben and Axl made more noise when they left the house than when they had entered. The brothers had carried out their assault on Magd in a near silence, speaking in whispers.

Igor was only half asleep when he heard Magd's door shut, footsteps on the stairs and the front door closing. He realised the noise was being made by more than one person and his thought was that it was Magd and the girl. As he left his bedroom to investigate he heard Magd groaning from the landing above.

Igor helped Magd as far as he could with painkillers and by dressing his smashed fingers. There was blood on the floor, on the bed in Magd's room, on a small hand towel and the room was a mess.

Igor realised that the only chance he had of saving the mission was to get out of Bovey Castle as soon as possible. He left Magd drinking whisky to dull the pain and went to the other two lodges to tell the diver and angling teams to get ready to leave right then before daylight.

Igor and Akram, the diver, cleaned up Magd's room, removed tell-tale items like the whisky, June's wine bottle, the amyl nitrate bottle and the bloodied hand towels. Then they all went carefully through the three Row C lodges, double-checking that nothing had been left which would help incriminate them.

Russia One, Arab One and Arab Two were all on the move by 05:30 driving in a loose convoy from Bovey Castle to the services area at Exeter on the western end of the M5 motorway.

Igor knew they had to move and regroup, and he needed to think. The hotel might inform the police there had been an incident in the Row C lodges, the girl's family might call the police to report Magd's attack, and the media could get hold of the story. These and other possibilities made Igor realise that they could soon be the object of an investigation, and a party of seven Syrians and a Russian would stand out and promote curiosity.

Igor had left an envelope in his lodge addressed to "The Manager, Bovey Castle Hotel." In the note he explained that unfortunately two of the men in the Syrian group had got drunk and had a fight over a game of cards. Their holiday was now over and everyone was going home. They had paid for the three lodges in advance and now left another £5,000 in cash saying that he hoped it would cover any damage or inconvenience. Igor knew his story was weak and full of holes but it was the only strategy he could come up with in a hurry.

He would never know it but his ploy worked. At an early morning meeting Bovey Castle's management decided to keep the money and say nothing, because at the beginning of the summer holiday season they did not want to report an incident they didn't understand to the police and risk the bad publicity that might result.

June Symonds's mother called the hotel and said her daughter was having a very bad monthly period and would not be coming to work for two days. When June did reappear she told one or two staff members that she had had a bad fight with her boyfriend.

Magd was silent as they drove towards the Exeter Services. Igor had often used the tactic of hiding in plain sight and this was what he was now trying to do. The services would not yet be busy, but as the day woke up there would be an increasing number of people using the facilities and there would be enough vehicles in the car park for their vehicles to not stand out.

The only contact he had had with the Russian Embassy in London was to collect a package which had been left for him at the Cumberland Hotel. This had been an emergency set of ID documents for the whole group including passports and UK driving licences, two sets of credit cards, one each for him and Magd in the names of their new ID's, £10,000 in crisp new notes and a Visa credit card for each of the Syrians backed by the Ahli United Bank in Kuwait.

Sitting in the Costa Coffee area of Exeter Services Igor gave his orders and outlined the plan. They would split up for three days and as long as nothing adverse happened and nothing appeared on the TV, radio news, or internet news feeders, they would meet for lunch three days later at the White Hart Hotel in Okehampton and compare notes. As long as no one had anything of concern to report they would then move to Bude and carry on with the operation as originally planned.

Igor told the anglers to go to Brixham as planned and find a place to stay and do their two days' sea fishing as booked. He told them to pay for accommodation for each man separately and use the new credit cards, but to pay for all incidentals in cash.

The diving team offered that there were several reef dives off Plymouth; they suggested they go there to try out all the new kit they had bought. Magd gave each team £2,000 in cash and by 08:00 two vehicles were going in different directions as part of the day's normal rush hour traffic.

Igor would leave the services a short while later; he had decided he wanted to be near Bude, so he called the Wellington Hotel in Boscastle and booked rooms for two nights.

After breakfast at the hotel Alexei and Yevgeny decided to go for a walk in Bovey Castle's grounds. They had found out that Igor's party was staying in three lodges in Row C and wanted to check out the lie of the land. There were no cars outside the lodges and cleaning staff could be seen in two of the three lodges. Their targets had disappeared and, back in the hotel, they contacted Moscow asking for guidance.

Handy Andy had the footage from his cameras outside the Row C lodges playing while he was getting up and getting ready to leave for another day at Bovey Castle. There was no camera in Magd's room, so he didn't know about the rape, or Reuben and Axl calling on the Syrian. However, the downstairs camera and the outside camera had filmed enough to clearly show there had been a lot of action in the night and all eight of their targets had now left Bovey Castle.

Andy called Gerald. "Boss, there seems to have been lots going on at Bovey last night, and I think our birds have flown, so no hurry to get there today."

Gerald told him to meet for breakfast ASAP.

By the time they met, Andy had looked at his trackers and was able to tell Gerald that all three of Igor's vehicles were stationary at the Exeter services area on the M5.

14

Gerald, Maddie and Andy were at breakfast long before the others. Andy had two laptops set up in front of them. One screen showed three dots side by side which were Igor's cars parked at the services and the other showed the footage which had been recorded by the cameras at the Row C lodges.

Maddie had rung around telling everyone that they could have a little lie-in because the early departure to Bovey Castle was off, and there would be a meeting over breakfast at 08:00 to discuss new developments. Curiosity as to what the new developments might be meant that no one had a lie-in, and by 07:30 the whole group was at breakfast speculating what might have happened.

There was no audio good enough to tell them exactly what had occurred, but it was obvious there had been two incidents which were connected. Bad audio from the downstairs bugs in Igor's lodge and the footage from the cameras had recorded June entering and leaving, a scream, Igor's raised voice and the sounds of discord and then a while later the arrival and departures of Reuben and Axl.

Gerald was starting to outline a plan of action to investigate what had happened when Andy cut in, "They are on the move, Boss."

Everyone crowded around Andy and watched the red dots representing Arab One and Arab Two move and then stay together for a while before going in different directions. Initially they went to the end of the M5, and then Arab Two carried on westward on the A38 towards Plymouth, and Arab One turned onto the A380 heading for Torbay. The third red dot was Igor's vehicle which didn't move for another half an hour. When he did move he also headed west but took the A30 towards Okehampton.

Gerald watched Igor's dot on the screen. "I would bet he is heading for Bude. We are a little blind at the moment and we need to do something about that. Richard, you, Ox, Andy and Jackie go after Arab One, follow them until they settle somewhere; then report and head back here. Christine, do the honours with Arab two, please. Maddie and I will head for Bovey and sniff around, and then we'll see where Andy says Igor has got to before we decide what to do about him."

After the two Syrian groups had left Igor logged into the services wi-fi via his VPN and sent a report to Moscow, which was a carefully considered version of the previous night's events. He had to report to Moscow; he couldn't avoid telling the truth, but the report he sent emphasised his belief that ultimately the operation had not been fatally compromised by Magd's actions. He told Moscow that the group had split into three and would not get back together until he was sure there would be no consequences which might adversely affect the outcome of the mission. Fifteen minutes after sending his report Igor received a message from the FSB agreeing that he should proceed as he suggested.

Alexei and Yevgeny had contacted Moscow fifty minutes after the FSB had received Igor's report. Their orders were to stay at Bovey Castle and wait to be told where Igor and Magd had gone. They were advised this might take a few days and were told to use the time to check around and clarify what had happened to make Igor move his group in a hurry. They were also told to keep their ears and eyes open for any gossip which might be going around the hotel, and especially if they heard the police might get involved.

Richard's group followed Arab One to Brixham where they checked in to the Berry Head Hotel before walking to the harbour. Once they were clear of the hotel Andy went in, and using a false ID which described him as a private detective he found out from the receptionist that the angling group had booked into the hotel for three nights. A short discussion in Jackie's VW produced the consensus that the anglers were obviously going ahead with their fishing charter. Richard rang Gerald to report and Gerald confirmed his earlier order to keep an eye on the anglers for the afternoon, then return to Tiverton.

The MI6 group headed for Plymouth where Arab Two's tracker guided them to the Crown Plaza Hotel where they found the divers' vehicle in the hotel parking. When they saw the Syrians emerge from the hotel and start walking, Christine and George followed them, using a leap frog approach so that neither of them was behind the divers for more than two or three hundred yards. It was just over a mile walk along the street to Sutton Harbour where the divers went into the blue-fronted Aqua-nauts shop.

Christine kept her distance while George hung around in

the shop pretending interest in several items. The divers told the shop manager they were interested in diving local sites and asked for advice. George had been around when the divers were in the shop previously, and didn't want to push his luck, so left as soon as he knew what the divers were doing. Christine called Gerald and reported in, and as with Richard's team, was told to return to Tiverton as soon as they were sure the divers were staying in Plymouth.

At Bovey Castle Gerald produced a press card and Maddie showed a press photographer's ID at reception. They asked to see the manager. They told the manager they were following up on a police report about a lodge let to a foreign tourist group which had been broken into last night.

The manager had only recently come out of a meeting at which it had been decided to play the incident down, so he wasn't aware of any police report, but said he would check and if he came up with anything, would let Gerald know. On their way out of the hotel Maddie chatted to Frankie Pinter, the woman at the reception desk who said she had heard the Arabs had been fighting and left in a hurry.

Gerald and Maddie drove away and Gerald made a mental note that Andy should return to the hotel the next day, pretending interest in a holiday lodge and remove his cameras. The cameras would be easy because they were outside, but a diversion might be needed if a member of staff accompanied Andy into Igor's lodge. Gerald decided that Christine should go with Andy to divert attention and allow him to remove his kit unseen.

That Christine was highly intrigued by the group she was working with was evidenced by her endless questioning of Andy the next day when they drove to Bovey Castle to remove his surveillance equipment. Her questioning was discreet and low key but persistent, and Andy often gave answers specifically designed to wind her up.

On more than one occasion she spotted this and glanced at him with a look that said, "If you think I believe that you are mad."

By pretending interest in renting lodges for a family occasion they were shown around the Row C lodges; Christine did a great job of holding the attention of the accompanying staff member and this enabled Andy to remove all his kit and put it out of sight in his ruck sack.

They decided to have a drink in the bar before leaving and struck gold. June was not expected back at work for another day and a Welshman called Dylan was doing double shifts at the bar, covering much of the day as well as June's evening shift. Dylan liked to talk and liked to think he was in the know regarding what really went on at the hotel.

Christine's skillful prodding hadn't got her very far with Andy, but it worked well on Dylan. He had heard rumours that June had been beaten up by her boyfriend which was why she wasn't at work, and that the fight among the Arabs had been caused by June because two of them fancied her. In a hushed voice he whispered across the bar counter to Christine that June's boyfriend heard that she had had a drink with the Arabs, accused her of having had sex with one of them, and beat her up. Dylan was putting two and two together and making five, but had latched onto some elements of what had happened.

When Christine later recounted her conversation with Dylan to Gerald he remarked that he thought Dylan's version might not be a million miles from the truth. Their targets had now moved and it seemed there would be no police involvement in whatever happened; so Gerald told Christine to tell Ros they wouldn't spend any further time investigating, but would focus on keeping close tabs on Igor's group. He asked Christine to re-inforce to Ros that it was now more important than ever that if the Moscow source reported anything regarding Igor's changes of plan, Ros must tell Gerald immediately.

Before dinner Alexi and Yevgeny had a drink in the bar and for the second time that day Dylan had an audience keen to listen to his now not so top secret theories about June and the hurried departure of the Syrian group.

The story took less than 24 hours to go full circle, because Alexei reported it to the FSB controller in Moscow, who then mentioned it in a meeting attended by Ros's Moscow mole who wasted little time reporting to Ros. Ros was hardly able to keep the chuckle out of her voice when, on a "guess what" basis, she reported the story to Gerald.

Provided there were no comebacks from Magd's actions Igor decided they would all relocate to Bude in three days, but he didn't want to go there immediately and be on the spot in case there were any adverse developments. He decided to stay close to Bude at Boscastle for the next two days while they kept their eyes and ears open, looking for any news media reports, and Magd recovered from his injuires.

When he had called the Wellington Hotel in Boscastle he booked rooms in the names of the new identities they were now using.

15

The *Annie Mae* was an 18-metre (60 foot) Dublin-registered ocean-going trawler skippered by a predatory-looking Greek called Nicholas Pandelis. Pandelis commanded a mixed crew of twelve Irish, Filipino, English and Greek sailors. They all shared one thing in common: they were unprincipled rogues who were not choosy about how they made a living.

Pandelis had never been aware of the identity of his charterers when the FSB had used him on three previous occasions, twice to smuggle weapons and once to land a covert FSB task force into a West African country.

A week earlier the *Annie Mae* had a rendevouz in the North Sea with a Russian trawler. A mixture of 15 different-sized boxes had been transferred from the Russian ship to the Irish one. The boxes contained an assortment of equipment, including automatic weapons, drones, explosives, RPGs, missiles and the various other items Magd had asked for and the FSB planners had thought might be needed for the attacks.

The crew of the *Annie Mae* didn't know what was in the boxes and didn't particularly care. Each crew member knew this was a special trip, and each man would be paid a $10,000 bonus on top of their share of the value of the catch.

To make money and for the sake of appearances, they would often trawl and add the catch to the fish already stored in the freezers, fridges and chillers in their holds.

After taking these mysterious boxes on board and hiding them among ice and dead fish in the holds, Captain Pandelis had been ordered to steam across the north of Scotland, and then south, down the west side of Britain, through the Celtic Sea, and then to fish, or pretend to fish, off the North Cornwall and North Devon coasts until he received further orders. In addition to the $10,000 bonuses being paid to each crew member, Pandelis was to get a bonus of $25,000 and the *Annie Mae*'s owners would receive $150,000 on top of all the fuel and other costs of the trip. The main reason to fish off the British coast was to provide cover and explain their presence in the area.

When attacking Magd's hands and face Reuben had not intended to be merciful. Magd had suffered agonising pain and there had been a lot of blood, but over the next few days, as the swelling went down, the cuts healed and the bruising changed colour and started to fade, it became apparent that he hadn't been as badly injured as first appearances had suggested.

After the diving and angling teams had left the Exeter Services heading for Brixham and Plymouth, Igor spent some time discussing his next move with an unresponsive Magd, who was not only in physical pain, but was also having to come to terms with a serious blow to his pride.

Igor's next destination would be Bude to do the final work before carrying out the attacks. He had always planned to move his group to Bude just before the attacks but now decided to get there earlier. However, until he could be sure that there would be no news or police activity following Magd's incident with the girl, he had decided not to stay in Bude but to stay somewhere close by, from where he could easily visit the Bude area and keep his ears and eyes open for any media or police interest in Magd's untimely sexual adventure.

Igor phoned the Wellington Hotel in Boscastle and booked

three rooms. He had no reason to believe he would need the third room, but a lifetime of working in the field had taught him to always make arrangements which enabled various options. He had told the Wellington that he and his friend would be arriving in the middle of the afternoon, which meant he was able to take as much time as he liked for the sixty mile drive.

He drove down the A30 to just past Launceston, then he turned right onto the A395, heading west to North Cornwall. He was careful to keep well within the speed limits not wanting to risk any possibility of being stopped by the police.

For most of the journey Magd maintained his morose glum silence. Magd was lucky because Igor had brought some codeine tablets with him to the UK. Codeine is a powerful opiate drug which is only available in Britain on prescription. Had Igor not had codeine with him Magd would have had to rely on much less powerful painkillers like paracetamol and aspirin which are available over the counter in British chemists.

One of the boxes on board the *Annie Mae* did contain a full emergency medical kit, including injectable morphine. Morphine would have eliminated the pain in Magd's smashed fingers, but no one had foreseen there would be a need for emergency supplies before the teams went into action to carry out the attacks. That Magd's sexual appetite would jeopardise the operation and produce an early need for medical items, could not have been foreseen during the planning stages. Igor had no sympathy with Magd for the pain in his hands, as he was still furious that he had threatened the whole operation.

They stopped at the Wilsey Down Inn in Hallworthy, and Magd drank three brandies, which was an indication of the level of pain he was still feeling in both hands despite his regular intake of codeine.

Having left the A39 main highway, Igor took the B3263 to Boscastle. The last few miles of the drive were slow due to having to follow a tractor for a couple of miles, and near to Boscastle the road was often so narrow that vehicles couldn't move in opposite directions, but had to pull in and wait for oncoming traffic to pass. The delays made Magd more bad-tempered which didn't displease Igor!

Boscastle is a very picturesque Cornish village with some 800 permanent residents. The village is popular with tourists and in holiday times its shops, pubs, hotels and guest houses do brisk business. The village had made world news in 2004 when a freak rainstorm caused a flood so violent that parked cars were swept from the centre of the village, past the little harbour, down the narrow inlet and out to sea.

Igor drove into the village early on a bright sunny summer's day and had no trouble finding the Wellington Hotel as it occupies a dominant position on the left of the main road in the centre of the lower part of the village. From there a track goes down to the harbour.

After they had checked in Magd told Igor he would spend the rest of the day and the night in his room catching up on sleep. Igor was quite relieved to see the back of his colleague for a while. He went for a walk past the Tourist Information Centre down to the little harbour; then had a coffee in a café from where he sent a message to Moscow with an up-to-date situation report, including that he had now arrived in Boscastle. Between six and seven that evening he watched both the BBC and ITV local news broadcasts and was relieved to see there were no mentions of the incident at Bovey Castle. Before having dinner in the hotel Igor called Vincent Headon in Bude and postponed the fishing trip he had booked for the next day, by one day .

After dinner on his way up to bed Igor went to Magd's room and knocked on the door. Magd took a while to open and Igor realised he had been asleep. Igor said he hoped Magd would feel better in the morning and told him to meet him for breakfast at 09:00 in the hotel dining room.

At breakfast the next morning Magd appeared to have almost fully recovered. There were new smaller dressings on his hands, he had shaved, bathed and after several hours' sleep, looked fully rested. The pain in his hands was now only a dull throbbing ache and this was slowly decreasing.

Once again Igor had monitored the news that morning and watched and listened to local radio and TV broadcasts before going to breakfast, and there was still no mention of Bovey Castle. He decided they would spend the day in Bude familiarising themselves with the layout of the town.

They set off going north up the A39 to Bude soon after breakfast. He parked in the Crescent Car Park near the canal bridge and walked across to the Falcon Hotel where he reserved a suite and a double room for two days later.

They had a coffee in the Brendon Arms next to the Falcon, and from there Igor called the diving group and the anglers and told both teams to meet him as planned in two days' time at the White Hart Hotel in Okehampton where he would brief them on the next phase of the operation.

From the Brendon Arms the pair walked up the Strand and stopped at the Premier Inn Hotel where Igor booked six rooms for the Syrians in two days' time. They walked all the streets in the small town, and then walked the streets on the other side of the golf course around which the town was built. In the afternoon they got into their hired vehicle and retraced all the routes they had covered on foot in the morning. It was unlikely they would ever need such extensive knowledge of Bude's streets, but Igor was a professional and as far as possible, liked to be prepared for anything.

The river Neet runs down the Strand in Bude where Magd's Syrian team stayed in the Premier Inn Hotel.

The tracking devices on Russia One and Arab One and Two meant that Gerald knew where his targets were, but didn't know what they were doing. At that night's evening meeting he told Richard to take his team to Boscastle early in the morning and keep eyes on Igor all day. He sent the MI6 team to Brixham to make sure the anglers were on their planned fishing trip, and said Maddie and he would head to Plymouth to check on the divers.

While Gerald was briefing his group a call came through from Ros on his burner phone.

"Where are you?"

After Gerald had explained that he was in the dining room in the main lodge in Tiverton Castle with the whole group Ros continued, "I had an interesting bulletin today via our Deep Throat. It seems that a fishing boat carrying all sorts of toys and goodies has been sent to RV off Bude with our friends. Furthermore, I hear that there is a pair of secret admirers who are tracking Igor and Magd, and will ensure their silence is golden after their job is finished. Lovely people. I will send a fuller explanation in safe gobbledygook to the office machine Christine has with her. Speak *bukra*."

Gerald had never understood why Ros sometimes injected random Arabic words into her conversations, bukra meant tomorrow, and either the word or the message had lit a fire under George.

"Wow, whizzo, so the game really starts, how exciting. Call the SAS and lock up your daughters."

This earned him a sharp, "Shut up, George!" from Christine; indulgent smiles from Richard and Ox, and a disbelieving look from Andy, who now put him back into the dangerous halfwit category. Maddie caught the vibes around the table and giggled.

Gerald continued, "So, whatever kit Igor and his boys need

for their attacks will almost certainly be transferred at sea, from the fishing boat to a vessel which will go out to meet them. They will almost certainly use the boat they bought from Rock Marine. And now we have a new dimension and another complication because it looks as if the Russians want to ensure Igor and Magd's silence by killing them after the operation. This thing is starting to take shape."

That the game was starting to take shape prompted a "Ripping stuff" remark from George before Gerald continued, "So now we will have four teams to keep tabs on. Good thing you brought two vehicles, Jackie. The two main takeaways are that, if possible, we must monitor the sea transfer of the kit, or at the very least, know when it happens, and once we have found them we will have to stay very close to our two new killer lover boys.

"These guys will have orders to take Igor and Magd out immediately after the job is done, but we must stop that, catch them and arrest them.

"Moscow will want them killed before they can talk, and from our side, this has to be prevented at all cost."

George couldn't resist following Gerald's briefing with a remark that everyone else around the table thought was ridiculous.

"Spiffing, can't wait, going to be great fun."

"You really are mad," said Andy.

"Probably," agreed George.

Gerald continued, "Once Igor and his boys are in custody, the risk to them will still exist if the killers are on the loose. We will have to devise a plan which will involve grabbing them, as well as all the others, immediately after the action. It would be nice to remove them earlier but if we do we will tip off Moscow and the Russians will certainly abort the mission. We have two killers on the loose but we don't know who they are, or where they are. Hopefully Ros will fill in some blanks soon, but from now on, we need to be super cautious and be looking out for a pair of hoods who will be tracking our targets alongside us."

16

For Gerald the game had moved up a gear the previous evening when Ros mentioned the two Russian assassins and the imminent arrival of Igor's equipment by sea.

Gerald had taken Richard and Ox back to his room and given each of them a 9 mm Glock 19 automatic pistol with ammunition for the 15-round magazine as well as a spare magazine for each weapon.

The next morning Gerald split Richard's group into two and sent them both to North Cornwall. Jackie was sitting in his special souped-up VW van with Richard, and behind them in the layby on the A39 Ox sat at the wheel of the Range Rover. Andy was sitting in Ox's vehicle with his laptop on his knees, keeping track of the opposition.

Andy watched as Igor's vehicle made its way very slowly along the B3263 from Boscastle towards where they were parked on the A39, waiting. When Igor's vehicle came into view Ox pulled out in front of it and Jackie then followed behind. Both vehicles kept their distance.

All Gerald's people appreciated that Igor was a trained intelligence officer and would spot a tail unless great care was taken. To avoid any risk of Igor realising he was being followed, they used a leapfrog technique and sometimes Ox was in front with Jackie behind and other times they swapped positions. They both overtook him before they got to Bude and were waiting for him when he turned off the A39. They then followed him to the canal basin where he parked.

Igor and Magd were each carrying a small rucksack as they walked along the canal basin towards the sea before crossing at the lock gate bridge. On the other side of the bridge they stood waiting until Vincent Headon, the harbour master, drove by and parked on the beach at the bottom of a slope which led down from the road. Igor and Magd walked down the slope to join the man they had chartered for their day of sea fishing.

After breakfast and before they all left for the day's work Maddie had approached Christine and asked if, now that the game had changed, she would like a handgun. Christine hesitated because there were only supposed to be three weapons among the group.

George had overheard and joined them, answering for Christine with an enthusiastic "Yes, great stuff." So, rather than have a gun end up in George's hands Christine agreed to take Maddie's SIG P365 and deliberately didn't ask whether it was legal. As long as she didn't know whether it was illegal she could always pretend she had assumed it was legal. Non-lethal self-defence weapons are legal in South Africa, and Gerald and Maddie had brought back several stun guns over the years.

All ten members of the group now carried an eight inch long black cylinder which looked like a torch but was actually a powerful stun gun. Having the stun gun in his inside jacket pocket had slightly mollified George, but nevertheless, he would have been much happier with the pistol Christine now carried in her shoulder bag. The use of firearms was an absolute last resort and issuing the firearms and stun guns was something that Gerald had not planned to do until the end of the game when Igor and his men were arrested. Even at this point Gerald had not expected anyone in his group would get into a position where a weapon would be needed.

Ros's plan was that all Igor's men would be kept under close surveillance and at the last minute when Gerald was sure the attacks were about to be executed, and Igor's men were in possession of incriminating weapons and explosives, Gerald would blow the whistle and the interception and arrest would be carried out by armed police supported by special forces. This had changed now that they knew there were two armed killers in the mix. Gerald was concerned that he knew nothing about what this new threat might involve, and issuing firearms and stun guns earlier than planned was a precautionary measure he could take.

Despite being a diver and enjoying being at sea Magd always approached sea trips with some anxiety because he was often violently seasick. Vincent Headon paddled out to his boat *Mantra* in a small dinghy, watched by Igor and Magd. After a few minutes' preparation he started Mantra's engine and moved to the small stone quay below the lock gates to pick up his clients. They left the quay and started out to sea after the tide had turned and was on its way out. This meant they had to spend the whole day at sea before the tide went back up the beach and enabled *Mantra* to get back onto the quay.

Igor did not want to display too much interest in the satellite dishes and make Vincent suspicious. He mentioned that they were staying in Boscastle and asked if they could go there just to see what the entrance to Boscastle looked like from the ocean.

On the way back across Bude Bay they headed for the satellite dishes while stopping a few times to fish for mackerel. Igor wanted to spend time having a good look at the GCHQ satellite dishes from the sea; so when they were about 500 yards off the cliffs in front of the dishes he suggested they use the mackerel they had caught as chum, and set up to see if they could catch a porbeagle shark. Igor hadn't thought about how they would set up a chum trail, so it was lucky that Vincent was a shark angler himself and had some onion bags on board which he used for chum and now filled with mashed up mackerel and hung over the side to set up a scent trail. Chum is known as rubby-dubby among Cornish shark anglers, and so for a few minutes Magd was confused that Igor kept referring to chum, while Vincent seemed to be talking about something else called rubby-dubby.

Vincent picked up on his confusion and explained that the two terms both referred to the same thing. The chum trail went well out to sea, and as Igor watched the two shark lines in the water he was hoping for a bite. They didn't have a bite in the two and a half hours they spent near the GCHQ station, but both Igor and Magd took several photographs and thoroughly observed the satellite dishes and the cliffs and the beach below.

They returned to harbour late in the afternoon and invited Vincent to have a drink with them in the Brendon Arms Pub. Vincent dropped Igor and Magd on the quay and joined them in the pub half an hour later after he had secured *Mantra* on her mooring, shut everything down, locked his wheelhouse and paddled back to shore.

Igor told Vincent that they had had a great day, and would be spending time on holiday in and around Bude and so would soon charter him again. Igor added an extra £50 tip to Vincent's fee for the day to help ensure his availability when needed in the future.

Weapons, explosives and combat were more in Magd's area of expertise than Igor's. On the drive back from Bude to Boscastle they chatted about how to carry out the attack from the sea. Magd had become convinced that the best chance of success would be to use two attack methods.

On board *Annie Mae* there were three different types of drone which were theoretically capable of being flown onto targets protected by radio jamming systems, and there were also four Javelin shoulder-fired anti-tank guided missiles. Javelins are American missiles made by Lockhead Martin which the Russians had acquired on the black market. The Javelin is one of the best weapons in its class in the world. The Russians had obtained the weapon because they wanted to study it to use the technology in developing a similar missile of their own, or upgrading their existing weapons to give them the same capabilitiy. Magd believed that the angler crew of three should first kill or otherwise incapacitate Vincent, and then use both weapon options to attack the site.

Once the attack had been launched the anglers would clear the area fast to rendezvous with the *Annie Mae* several miles offshore. They would then scuttle *Mantra* and dump Vincent's body before boarding the Irish vessel and making their escape. Vincent's body being in the same area as the wreckage of *Mantra* would tie in and give authorities a logical conclusion if any wreckage from the boat was found.

While everything they had observed was fresh in their minds Igor and Magd developed the plan, and while Igor drove back to Boscastle Magd made cryptic entries in Arabic in his notebook.

All three of the anglers had flown drones but this didn't negate the need for experience and training on the actual drones they would fly. Neither Igor, Magd or any of the anglers had ever seen a Javelin, so as well as training on the drones, they would also need to familiarise themselves with the operation of the missiles.

When they got back to Boscastle Igor contacted the anglers and the divers and instructed them to meet him as planned in Okehampton the next day. He then reported to his FSB/SVR controllers and informed them he would take delivery of the boat they were buying in the next couple of days. He asked that the Irish vessel be contacted to find out when she would arrive off North Cornwall, and so that a time for a rendezvous at sea could be arranged. He also informed his control that he planned to leave Boscastle the next day and relocate the whole group to Bude.

Magd's injured hands and bruised ego were now almost healed and Igor's anger at his colleague's indiscretion had subsided.

They were a working team again, and when they strolled down to Boscastle's little harbour after dinner at the Wellington, the mood was light and the camaraderie had returned. They agreed that they expected to have the job done and be out of Britain within a couple of weeks at most.

Richard and Jackie had passed the day killing time in the Bude harbour area, waiting for Igor and Magd to return on *Mantra* with Vincent. Ox and Andy were also killing time walking the cliffs to the north of Bude. They hadn't planned on keeping an eye on *Mantra*, but fortunately it had worked out that way. At various times Ox had called Richard to report he had *Mantra* in sight through his binoculars. They were walking back from having had tea at a little café at Northcott Mouth when Ox saw the *Mantra* about five hundred yards offshore steaming back towards Bude harbour.

Ox called Richard and Andy who were sitting in the Olive Tree in the canal basin having a glass of wine. Thirty-five minutes later Richard and Andy watched Igor and Magd walk up the other side of the canal and go into the Brendan Arms Pub, where they were soon joined by Vincent Headon.

When they left the Brendon Arms Richard called Gerald and said they would follow Igor and Magd on the tracker, and as long as they headed back to Boscastle Richard suggested there was no point in continuing to tail. Gerald agreed and told him if that was the case, then they should all drive back to Tiverton Castle.

Twenty minutes after Richard had reported in, Christine called Gerald from Brixham to say that her anglers were back onshore and in their hotel. Like Richard she was also told to head back to the base in Tiverton.

Moscow is two hours ahead of London and it was 9:00 pm when the joint FSB/SVR control received Igor's report. He had outlined his plan for the attacks and all those involved in the Moscow end of the operation were summoned to FSB headquarters on Lubyanka Square in the Meshchansky District of Moscow for a meeting an hour and a half later at 10:30 Moscow time.

The meeting lasted an hour; an hour later Ros received a report from her source and immediately called Gerald.

"Another bulletin from Chatterbox, things are speeding up all the time. Iggy Pop is moving to Buddy tomorrow with all his guys. His two secret admirers are called Yevgeny and Alexei and they have been told to get to Buddy in the next couple of days, hang around and await further orders. It seems that before leaving Bovey for Buddy they must wait for a special package which is being delivered to them from London. I would think this will be the kit they need for sending Iggy Pop and Maggie to slumberland. The last item of interest is that our pirate fishing boat is not called the *Jolly Roger* but the *Annie Mae*. She has been told to motor to Buddy with all speed.

"I will get in touch with our MOD contact and ask him to have a team from Hereford or Poole* on standby, starting a few days from now. Have a think and have a chat with the guys and get back to me. One decision will be when to move to Buddy, and I guess another is that you should have a boat nearby which you can access."

To any chance eavesdropper Ros's use of Buddy for Bude, Chatterbox, Iggy Pop and Maggie would have been baffling nonsense but Gerald immediately knew who and what she was referring to. They closed the call and Gerald said he would get back to her within an hour.

Hereford is the home of the SAS, and Poole is the Headquarters of the Special Boat Squadron, the SBS, which is the Royal Navy's equivalent of the SAS.

Gerald called everyone together and led a team meeting to discuss the developments Ros had reported. Gerald and Maddie could have moved back to their house in Bude, however, not only did Igor know which house it was, which might mean he looked at it from time to time, but if they were continually in Bude it would increase the chance of Igor seeing them. The plan was that Gerald would be on the spot when Igor was arrested and would be in charge of handling him and explaining the MI6 propositions. But unless something unforeseen happened which made it a good move for Gerald to contact Igor earlier, he needed to stay out of sight while still keeping as close to the Russian as possible.

Gerald decided that Richard, Ox, William and Henry would move to Bude the next day in the MI6 VW van full of its electronic wizardry. Maddie, himself, Andy, Jackie, Christine and George would, for the time being, remain based in Tiverton and commute as necessary to Bude which is only 63 miles away, and would take less than an hour and a half without traffic; an hour and forty-five minutes when it was busier.

This gave Gerald two armed men on the spot keeping surveillance on the opposition, supported by two electronics people. During the day, or when otherwise needed, the Bude team could be reinforced from Tiverton and the two teams could be swapped over and alternated if required.

Maddie made a call to her friend, Stefanie Tanner, who ran the Brendon Arms next to the Falcon Hotel in Bude. She had two requests. She asked Stefanie to use her influence with the hotel next door to get four rooms if possible, but said if this wasn't, then two rooms which could be shared, would be fine. Her second request was that Stefanie email her the guest list for every day starting the next day. This request was not something Stefanie should have agreed to due to data protection and client confidentiality, but she knew that Maddie would not be asking without a good reason.

The email came back ten mintes later. Maddie read it on her phone, smiled, looked at Gerald and said, "Bingo, what a jolly little coincidence! Stefanie has got us four rooms at the Falcon, and it seems that Richard, Ox, William and Henry will be sharing the hotel with Igor and Magd."

Gerald wasn't quite so amused and immediately set about questioning Richard, Ox, William and Henry as to whether they thought Igor or Magd might have seen them before and remembered it. William and Henry were immediately off the hook because when surveillance operations had been running, they had always been out of sight in the MI6 VW van.

Richard and Ox agreed that although Igor and Magd might have seen them at some time there was no reason why they should be remembered. Richard pointed out that he had been hanging around the Falcon area both before and after Igor and Magd had gone fishing, but he didn't think it mattered because he was just another holidaymaker in the Falcon Hotel, so it was normal to be seen from time to time.

With a plan in place and the accommodation sorted out Gerald had one more call to make before he contacted Ros. Maddie and he kept an eight metre Ribeye boat called *Glauca* with twin 250cc Suzuki engines in Padstow. Cole Benson was a Bude sea-angling skipper, a sometime builder and an old friend of Gerald's.

The call he had from Gerald intrigued him. Gerald had asked him to take a few days off and go fishing using *Glauca*. He offered Cole £300 a day to go to Padstow every day for the next week or so and leave Padstow as early each morning as the tide allowed and steam to offshore Bude and hang around all day fishing as he liked and wait for Gerald's call, which might or might not happen.

Cole and his cell phone were often not in the same place at the same time; so Gerald gave him a firm instruction that he was always to have his phone with him, and as far as possible, he was always to be in places with a good cell phone signal.

Only half joking Gerald told Cole that £100 would be deducted from his pay every time he tried to call Cole but didn't get an answer.

Cole knew Gerald's boat and had a set of keys because when Gerald was out of Cornwall, Cole kept an eye on the boat for him. £300 daily to sit in a boat off Bude fishing all day was Cole's idea of a good career move. He said he would start the job in two days' time and finished with, "I won't ask what's going on if you promise you'll tell me one day."

Gerald replied, "Sorry, I won't promise and I probably won't tell you."

Cole chuckled. "Up to no good, I bet. Alright, mate, nice one, just make sure it's cash."

Gerald finished his day by calling Ros and explaining all his arrangements. The MI6 agent listened intently and when Gerald had finished, remarked, "That all sounds good. Well done. Approved. Two points, you are relying on Richard and Ox at the front end, things could get interesting. Are you sure they are any good, sure they can handle what might come?"

Gerald said, "The best, what's your next point?"

She replied, "This is the first time I have heard of Cole, what might he be like if he gets caught up in things going awry?"

Gerald thought that the words Cole and awry in the same sentence were probably quite appropriate but didn't say so. He replied, "He is Cornish, an ex-para, a rogue, a friend and I trust him, good enough?"

"That'll do," said Ros. "I am just beginning to get a good feeling about this one. I think we might just pull it off. Christ, I would pay a lot of money to see Vlad Putin's little fat round face when someone tells him we have foiled his operation."

"I think you will have to conjure up that image in your imagination. We will speak tomorrow, sleep well," and Gerald closed the call.

17

On their drive from Boscastle to Okehampton to meet the anglers and the divers it was Magd who came up with a planning consideration which hadn't been discussed before. He pointed out to Igor that the equipment on board the *Annie Mae* which they would soon take delivery of, would have to be unloaded secretly once they got it ashore, and might be bulky and require a storage area.

Igor was pleased that Magd was back, focused on the operation; the incident with the girl was now past history. Igor told Magd that while the question was something that needed addressing, it couldn't have been planned for in detail in advance because the circumstances hadn't been known. They would soon have the boat which the divers had bought and it had locking storage in which some equipment could be kept. They also had the three rental vehicles which all had locking boots and plenty of space inside them.

Igor explained that he had been considering these issues since they left Bovey Castle and he had been told the *Annie Mae* was on her way. He had initially thought of renting a holiday house or chalets which would give them storage space, but had discounted this because he thought that eight foreign men suddenly looking for holiday accommodation would attract more attention than staying in hotels and being part of guest lists. He also saw the advantage of having no cooking and cleaning to do, and being guests in hotels conformed to his hiding in plain sight strategy.

Magd saw the logic in not having rented a house and didn't comment further.

As part of his planning Igor had decided that both he and Magd would go to sea to meet the *Annie Mae*. They would unpack and inspect all the equipment while they were on board the fishing vessel. Magd would only select the equipment they would use in the GCHQ attack and the attack on the Google cable, and these would be the only items they would take back to shore with them.

Igor had put this plan to Moscow and it was approved, and Moscow confirmed that Igor should discard all the equipment he wasn't going to use over the side of the vessel. Moscow obviously didn't trust Captain Pandelis and his motley crew not to become gun runners if spare equipment gave them expensive items to sell and make a handsome profit.

Igor and Magd got to the White Hart Hotel in Okehampton earlier than expected. He left Magd in the hotel to wait for the diving team and the anglers while he walked to the nearby Pig Pen Café to send an update to Moscow. Before ordering his coffee and settling into a corner table he did his usual visual check to make sure there were no CCTV cameras in operation.

Andy was rarely very far from one of his screens on which he could track Igor's three vehicles, and William and Henry were linked in and also almost permanently kept an eye on the tracked vehicles.

William was at the breakfast table with one eye on his cornflakes and the other on his screen when he realised that all three of Igor's vehicles were on the move. Seconds later Andy appeared, carrying a laptop.

"Where's the boss, all our friends are on the road and it

looks like they may be converging heading to a meet up?"

"Yup, I noticed as well," said William through a mouthful of cereal.

Gerald and Maddie joined the breakfast group a few minutes later, and as the minutes ticked by, it did indeed look as if all three vehicles were heading for a meeting point: The divers cleared Plymouth and headed north on the A386 towards Tavistock, the anglers were moving north on the A380 and Igor was moving west heading inland on the A395.

They watched and Gerald spoke first. "The trackers are great but they only tell us where these guys are, and we don't know where they are finally heading. Without eyes on, we won't know what they are doing when they get there. We'll take Arab Two, Richard, you and Ox take Arab One, and Christine, you go after Igor. Andy will direct us as to intercept our targets. Ten minutes, everyone, in cars and moving, please."

They all moved off, having estimated where to intercept each target vehicle, while Andy kept advising Gerald and Richard where their targets were.

In the MI6 vehicle William sat next to Christine, directing her intercept of Igor.

It soon became clear that their guess had been correct and each of Igor's three vehicles were heading to a central point which looked as if it could be Okehampton.

Henry was taking advantage of the down time to play video games and George leant over the seat, looking over William's shoulder at the laptop on his knees. "Ripping, a reunion, looks like our three birds are all flying towards the same nest. I wonder what the hell they are going to do in Okehampton. Won't be any prostitutes there, I wouldn't have thought!" George sat chuckling at his own joke, Henry looked blank and Christine's eyes rolled in her head.

George wasn't finished and said to Christine, "Guns are not

so much a chick thing as they are for men; so if you would feel happy giving me your pistol, old girl, then feel free, what!"

"George, think carefully, if you have just referred to me as a chick and an old girl, then you might want to consider jumping out now, because when we stop I am going to break your fucking neck, you posh little twit."

Henry stopped playing his video game, William shot Christine a sideways glance.

"Oops! Sorry, Boss. I didn't mean to offend. Just a bit of fun, tee hee."

"George, did you actually just say tee hee? No, don't answer; just sit back in your seat and shut up. I don't want to hear from you again until we get to wherever we are going, and even then silence would be a blessing."

An hour later Gerald's three vehicles were parked side by side in the Waitrose car park in Okehampton. The trackers told them that Igor, Arab One and Arab Two were all parked in Simmons' car park. There weren't many places in Okehampton where Igor could be meeting his people.

Neither Gerald, Maddie, Richard or Ox could afford to be recognised by Igor, so Christine, George, Andy and Jackie set out on foot to check out the hotels, cafés and restaurants in the small town. George spotted the three divers standing outside the White Hart Hotel smoking. When the divers went into the hotel, George asked if someone else could go into the hotel to see if they were all there. George had twice been in the diving shop in Plymouth with the divers and didn't want to get too close to them again and risk being recognised.

Gerald told Jackie to go and check the hotel, while everyone else went back to the Waitrose car park to await the outcome. Jackie joined the group in the car park fifteen minutes later and reported that Igor's whole team were in the hotel in the dining room, having coffee; they hadn't ordered yet, but he thought they were probably staying for lunch.

Gerald told Richard and Ox to head for Bude and settle into the Falcon Hotel. The MI6 team, Maddie and he left the centre of Okehampton and went to the Burger King at the Shell Services a few miles out of town on the A30, to await developments.

Jackie and Andy stayed in town, taking turns to keep Igor's group under surveillance. As expected they did stay for lunch in the hotel and then drove in a loose convoy to Bude, where the six Syrians checked into their rooms at the Premier Inn and Igor and Magd settled in across the bridge in the Falcon Hotel.

As soon as it was clear that their targets were all heading for Bude Gerald and Maddie went back into Okehampton to pick up Jackie and Andy.

Igor, Magd, the divers and anglers had been alone in the White Hart Hotel dining room, and when there were no waiters or waitresses around, Igor talked to his men in low tones. The six Syrians had been briefed on the objectives of the operation when Magd had recruited them in Damascus. Further information had been given to them in Doha before flying to London, and that was all they had needed to know then.

Igor outlined the whole plan in detail, and told his men that they would now move from Okehampton to Bude where they would be based for the rest of the operation. He outlined the role of the *Annie Mae*, including their escape plan.

He told them that having mounted their attacks, each team would leave the area and steam straight out to sea to rendezvous with the *Annie Mae*, where they would sink their boats. The *Annie Mae* would then take the men to Wexford in the Irish Republic. From Wexford the six men would travel to Dublin where they would split up and fly back to the Middle

East by various routes.

Igor further explained that the *Annie Mae* would arrive in the area in the next few days. He told the divers to go to Padstow the next day and take delivery of their boat. They would then spend the rest of the day and the day after fully familiarising themselves with their new vessel so that they would be ready to head out to sea to meet the *Annie Mae* as soon as she arrived.

Although the divers would be operating the boat Igor told the anglers to also spend time learning about the navigation equipment and other features, because after the attack on GCHQ they would need to be able to handle Vincent's boat for their getaway to meet the *Annie Mae*.

Of the three anglers Daoud was the most experienced with boats. He was keen to learn all he could about the local sea conditions and the equipment on board. The navigation and other equipment on their 6.5 metre Leeward and Vincent's boat *Mantra* would be very similar; so Daoud was keen to practise all he could.

Igor explained that once Magd had decided on the methods of attack and selected the equipment which would be used, time would then need to be taken training. Igor had booked an all day charter with Vincent for the anglers the next day, so while the divers were picking up their boat, the anglers would be building their cover with Vincent and getting to know him.

After lunch the six Syrians headed for Bude for the first time and on arrival checked into the Premier Inn.

Just before lunch, while Igor's team were having coffee in the White Hart Hotel, a special courier was delivering two padded packages to the reception of the Bovey Castle Hotel. The receptionist rang Alexei who said he would come and collect them immediately. Back in his room Alexei called Yevgeny and together they unpacked two Sig Sauer 9 mm pistols with ammunition, a sniper rifle with a folding stock, two knives with eight inch blades, wire garottes, syringes and four small glass phials containing clear liquid. The equipment had been sent by Moscow in the diplomatic bag, and had been chosen to give the killers various options when it became time to permanently silence Igor and Magd.

The two Russians had been packed and ready to leave as soon as their equipment was delivered. The hotel had agreed they could have late check-outs until 2:00 pm. At 1:40 pm they were on the road heading west to Tintagel where they would stay within striking distance of Bude and wait for further orders.

Cole Benson liked Gerald's 8.5 m Ribeye *Glauca*. If ever he acquired a rubber duck – which is what he called RIBs – instead of a hard boat, this would be the type he would have. He spent the day on preparations. He ran the engines up and checked everything, filled the fuel tank and put two spare tanks of fuel in one of the storage lockers. He then went for a short run out into the estuary to check everything again before deciding he was happy. He called it a day and drove home to Bude.

The next day he would catch the morning tide and steam up to Bude to start his £300 a day fishing holiday. Cole wasn't sure why but he had the feeling that the old adage, "Nothing ever happens in Bude", might be about to be proved wrong. He was not only a keen sea angler, he was also a keen hunter who had permission to shoot rabbits and vermin on several local farms. Due to these shooting activities he possessed a couple of shot-guns and a very powerful .22 air rifle. While driving back to

Bude, and for no reason, Cole decided that he would bring his shotgun with him every day when he was on standby off Bude in Gerald's boat.

The Camelot Castle Hotel in Tintagel had a number of East Europeans and Russians working as staff. Yevgeny and Alexei noted this and realised they would have to take care not to speak Russian in front of staff members who would recognise the language. They were travelling on Turkish passports, both spoke Turkish and they made a point of often speaking the language around the hotel when within earshot of others.

The killers had watched Igor and Magd arrive at Heathrow Airport, so knew what they looked like. From the next day on they would start to spend time in Bude familiarising themselves with Igor and Magd's routines and habits; the layout of the Falcon Hotel; Bude's streets and environs, and everything else they might need to know in a hurry when the time came to kill the Russian and the Syrian.

Events moved quickly the following morning. Richard and Ox called Gerald to report that Igor and Magd had met the anglers outside the Falcon Hotel at 9:00 and had strolled down to the harbour where they met Vincent Headon and went to sea.

Andy had been puzzled when, at 8:30 only one target vehicle moved which was Arab Two, the divers, and they headed south down the A39.

Gerald's guess was that they were going to Rock Marine to take delivery of their boat, but he needed eyes on to confirm this. Half an hour later Richard had reported from Bude that the other five had gone to sea which meant that he and Ox were free; so Gerald sent them on the short trip south to keep an eye on Arab Two, which Andy's tracker had confirmed had turned off the A39 at Wadebridge and was indeed heading for Rock.

Gerald called Cole Benson who had clearly heeded the warning about always having his cell phone with him and switched on because he answered immediately. Cole was steaming north from Padstow as instructed to take up his standby watch off Bude in Gerald's boat.

Gerald told Cole to keep heading for Bude and keep in touch because Maddie and he would need picking up off a Bude beach in a couple of hours.

The tide was three-quarters of the way out when Gerald and Maddie, both wearing wetsuits, waded out from Summerleaze Beach, each carrying a sealed dry bag, and then swam the remaining eighty yards to where Cole had anchored *Glauca* and sat waiting for them. They could see *Mantra*, Vincent's boat, in the distance to the north off Lower Sharpnose Point with the GCHQ dishes standing guard on the cliffs above. Gerald and Maddie had swum out to *Glauca* wearing goggles to partly obscure their faces.

They kept the goggles on and Gerald told Cole to move a couple of hundred yards away to the south where Maddie and he changed into the clothes in their dry bags and removed their swimming goggles. These precautions were in case Vincent looked through binoculars and recognised Gerald, Maddie and *Glauca*. If Vincent had mentioned to Igor that he knew the people in the RIB (rigid inflatable boat) over there, or even named Gerald and Maddie, then Igor might have been alerted that he was under surveillance.

Gerald and Maddie draped their wetsuits over the side obscuring the name *Glauca* and wore dark glasses and beanie hats while Cole kept the RIB at the limit of binocular range.

Gerald shadowed Igor all day while his party fished in various locations off Bude. Late in the afternoon Vincent took Igor and the Syrians back into Bude's little harbour and Cole steamed south towards Widemouth Bay where Gerald and Maddie swam ashore.

The MI6 team had spent the day in Bude on standby, and once Gerald and Maddie had changed back into dry clothes, Maddie called Christine to bring the VW van to Widemouth to give her and Gerald a lift back to their vehicle in Bude.

Richard and Ox had returned from Rock a short while earlier and the VW proved its worth as an out of sight meeting place when all eight in Richard's group crowded into the vehicle in the Crescent Car Park near the Falcon Hotel for a debriefing. Richard and Ox reported that the divers had taken delivery of their boat which was now at a berth they had rented from Rock Marine.

Gerald knew that keeping eyes on was the only way of knowing what Igor's group were doing, and so from then on the two VW vans, Maddie and he would rendezvous at seven-thirty every morning in the Crescent Car Park where the two vans could be parked side by side to serve as a local HQ and meeting point. In addition Andy would drive Jackie's Land Rover to the meeting point to increase their options to respond to whatever situations might arise.

On the right-hand side of the Falcon Hotel at first floor level there is a large open garden area. This outside area can be reached either by steps which lead up from street level or from within the hotel. When assessing the hotel Igor had picked the garden as a good area for holding meetings as long as the weather was dry.

The area had many advantages: there were two ways in and out, Igor could make sure his meetings were not overheard, there was a bar for refreshments, and with no walls or corridors no one could approach too closely unseen.

That evening the divers reported that the boat was now tied up at its quay in Rock, was fully fuelled and ready for use as soon as needed. Igor said he had heard that the *Annie Mae* would arrive off Bude the next day, and they would need to go from Padstow the day after to meet the fishing vessel and transfer equipment.

The divers talked of their day at sea fishing. Akram said he had observed Vincent closely and was totally confident of being able to operate *Mantra*. Igor confirmed that he had booked charters with Vincent every other day for the next week which would take them to the day GCHQ would be attacked.

Igor instructed everyone to be ready to leave Bude at eight the next morning when they would drive to Rock in two vehicles and spend the day at sea familiarising themselves with their new boat.

18

On April Fool's Day, 1st April 1939, a new anti-aircraft command facility came into being on the cliffs above Sharpnose Point. It was called RAF Cleave Camp. The camp was put to various uses during World War Two and afterwards, until the site was re-designated Composite Signals Organisation Station (CSOS), Morwenstow in the 1960s. The site became fully operational as an intelligence collection facility in 1974 and is now one of the most important intelligence assets working for the UK, the US and their allies. Cleave Camp, RAF Cleave, the Spy Centre, Cornwall's Society of Spies are all names which have been used to describe the site.

The Government Communications Headquarters (GCHQ) is often referred to as a jewel in the crown of the UK intelligence community. Perched as it is on the cliffs above Bude the antenna dishes are like eyes looking out to sea, guarding the UK's western approaches and searching the skies for enemies. September 2024 marked fifty years since GCHQ Bude became the world's first communications satellite (COMSAT) installation.

GCHQ Bude is not just of massive intelligence operational value, it also has huge symbolism for locals and visitors to North Cornwall who realise what it is. People look at the antenna dishes and feel reassured that their country has a first-class intelligence-gathering operation helping to keep them safe.

Igor's FSB and SVR controllers knew that to be successful, a strike against GCHQ didn't necessarily have to destroy too much of the site's operational capability. That would almost be a bonus, because just the fact that an unknown terrorist organisation had managed to launch an attack against the site would be a massive blow to British morale and national pride. The Islamic Peoples Front (IPF) would claim responsibility, and the Russians would ensure that there was no actual hard proof that their intelligence services had been behind it.

If it was suspected around the world that the Russians had been behind the attack, then this would boost Russian kudos. The aim was that there would only ever be suspicion but no hard proof. The sabotage of the Google Transatlantic Internet Cable would also be claimed by the IPF. The cable attack would be insurance in case the GCHQ attacks failed. It would further underline Britain's vulnerability as well as causing considerable disruption.

Igor was fully aware of the huge importance of the mission he was in command of. He also realised that both he and Magd might be at risk for the rest of their lives due to the knowledge they had. In the short term, if Russian involvement was proved, it could provoke a confrontation with NATO which could lead to war; in the medium and long term, if the truth came out, it would be a serious diplomatic embarrassment.

He had no idea that Yevgeny and Alexei were already in the area and their job was to ensure his and Magd's permanent silence. However, he fully recognised his vulnerability, and for this reason had decided to move to Canada and establish a whole new identity for himself and his family once the operation had ended and he had been paid. The large fee he would receive for this operation, together with the balance in his secret Austrian account would, he hoped, provide for his family for the rest of their lives.

Just like Igor, the FSB and SVR were aware of the importance of their plan, but so were Ros, MI6 and the British government. The stakes in the game could hardly have been higher for all the players. While Gerald and Maddie had been watching Igor's fishing trip with Vincent, Ros had spent the day in a succession of meetings in London. She had briefed her own management in MI6 and had also briefed officials in the Foreign, Commonwealth and Development Offices, the No. 10 Chief of Staff, and MI5.

Ros was under considerable pressure, not least because of the inclusion of Gerald and his team, and the unconventional way she was running the operation. She defended her position by pointing out that Gerald's inclusion might be decisive due to his past relationship with Igor, that Gerald knew the area of operations like the back of his hand, had useful local contacts and had an MI6 team attached to him.

Ros expressed confidence that Gerald's team and her MI6 people would be close enough to the opposition to ensure the attacks never happened. She assured her doubters that evidence would be gathered, arrests made and that Gerald was the best person to handle Igor and put their proposal to him.

Ros explained that the original objective of turning Igor and having him work as a double agent for MI6 had been abandoned as soon as it was realised that Moscow wanted him dead after the operation.

However, she believed that getting Igor's co-operation would now be easier once he knew his own side had planned to kill him. She didn't know that Igor planned to disappear with his family, but had she done so she would have seen this as giving her another strong card to play.

After getting back to Tiverton Castle Gerald had a long talk to Ros, using Christine's secure MI6 link. He confirmed that Igor's group now had a boat of their own, and also that it looked as if he planned to use Vincent in his operation. He assured Ros that with Cole Benson at sea and his group of ten people with five vehicles, he was confident he could keep eyes on the opposition, gather evidence and be able to warn Ros of any impending attack in time to deploy the police and special forces.

Gerald could sense that Ros was nervous and rightly guessed that she was under great pressure. One of the aspects that most concerned both Gerald and Ros was the presence of the two assassins.

For her part, Ros told Gerald that the *Annie Mae* was now under satellite surveillance, was closing in on Bude and would arrive offshore North Cornwall within twenty-four hours. Gerald was relieved to learn that Alexei and Yevgeny were staying in Tintagel. Not knowing where they were or what they were doing had been a continual concern in the back of his mind.

He told Ros that he would send Handy Andy and Jackie to Tintagel the next day to use Andy's long lenses to get photos of the killers and stay close to them all day in case they picked up anything useful.

Ros suggested that as soon as Gerald knew that Igor and Magd had left their rooms in the Falcon Hotel he should send her tech guys, William and Henry, to bug their rooms. Gerald queried how they would gain access to the rooms and, rather mysteriously, Ros told him not to worry about it!

Ros said she would be back in the Westcountry in two days and then planned to stay until the end of the operation. By the time they ended their chat Gerald sensed that Ros was far more relaxed and comfortable than she had been at the beginning.

Ros telling Gerald not to worry when he asked how William and Henry would gain access to Igor and Magd's rooms to bug them had piqued his curiosity. He went to the dining room area and found Christine and her team relaxing, having coffee while watching the film, *Jaws*, on the television.

When Gerald mentioned the need to bug the rooms and enquired about access, William told him that the hotel would lose its satellite TV signals and he and Henry would then turn up to fix it. Just like Ros, they were being deliberately mysterious, so Gerald had to push them.

Eventually William explained that they would block the hotel's satellite signals and all the TVs would fail. Then he and Henry would turn up, posing as engineers and fix the problem. During fixing it they would have the run of the hotel and would only need less than a couple of minutes to place listening devices in Igor and Magd's bedrooms and bathrooms.

When the explanation was over, George couldn't help but contribute, "Tip top, tip top, we'll be able to hear the buggers snoring and farting. Whizzo!"

Christine countered with, "If that is your idea of 'whizzo', George, I am sorry for you. Shut up and watch the film."

George was obviously bored and asked, "Anyone fancy going out for a beer? We could find a nearby hostelry and fraternise with the locals."

There was no answer and Gerald said, "Goodnight, every-one," over his shoulder as he left the room. George followed him and said, "Goodnight, Gerald," when they split up heading different ways. Gerald was making for his room and George was going to a quiet spot he had found where he could smoke a joint in peace without worrying about being caught and ad-monished by Christine.

That night everyone in Bude and Tiverton on both sides went to bed realising that the end game was creeping closer. Some were involved purely for the money, others were just doing their jobs, and in Gerald and Maddie's case, what they needed were challenges from time to time.

There were three players who were totally relaxed and unaffected by the slow increase of tension as each day went by: George was on his second marijuana spliff, watching swifts, swallows and martins circling and swooping in the sky above him, and Alexei and Yevgeny had long since stopped being affected by anything that life threw at them.

The main actors, all trying to stay ahead of the game, were now in the theatre, on the stage, or in their dressing rooms getting ready to play their parts. When the curtain went up and they met, the play would gather momentum as it moved towards a dangerous and dramatic finale. There would be no in betweens, only alive and dead, and winners and losers.

PART THREE

Staying Ahead of the Game

19

The Camelot Castle Hotel can be seen from Bude several miles up the Cornish coast to the north from where it looks as if someone has placed a matchbox on the cliff top.

Andy and Jackie did not know what Yevgeny and Alexei looked like, but they hoped the two Russians would be identifiable among the other guests at the hotel. To make sure the Russians would still be at the hotel when they got there, they left Tiverton at 07:00 and arrived at the Camelot Castle Hotel at 08:30.

Visitors have to pass through a turnstile to gain access to Reception and the rest of the hotel. Andy and Jackie entered separately and stayed apart to increase the chance to identify their targets. Would the two Russians look like Russians, would they speak Russian and would they be together? Andy and Jackie did not want to enquire about Yevgeny and Alexei, so were largely trusting to luck to be able to make the identifications.

Separately both asked Reception whether, as non-residents, they could have breakfast, were told yes, and Andy was the first to head for the dining room. They had pre-arranged that if either of them identified the Russians they would send an SMS to the other.

Andy sat at a table for two in the corner from where he could observe all those coming and going. Jackie didn't go straight to the dining room, but instead wandered around the ground floor, checking out all the public rooms before going into breakfast.

Jackie opted for the full works, a cooked breakfast of bacon, eggs, sausages, tomatoes and mushrooms while Andy chose yoghurt, muesli and a fruit salad. They were ignoring each other sitting at adjacent tables, and when Jackie's huge cooked breakfast arrived Andy glanced at him and raised an eyebrow.

Only two other tables were occupied by couples who weren't watching, and Jackie was mouthing, "You're just jealous," when two men entered. Neither Andy nor Jackie could have explained why they knew immediately that the pair were their targets but they were both sure of it and they were right.

Andy's breakfast had come from the buffet and he had not ordered anything else, so a couple of minutes after the Russians had walked in, he left more than enough money on the table to pay for his breakfast and left. He walked straight back to Reception and on the way took a £20 note out of his pocket. He held out the banknote and said to the receptionist, "I found this just outside the dining room, I think it might have been dropped by one of two German gentlemen who just went into breakfast."

The girl looked up and replied, "Thank you, Sir, I will ask. Actually I think they may be Russian, not German."

Andy gave her what he hoped was a dazzling smile and left the building through the turnstile heading to the car park. There were eleven cars in the car park. Andy had no way of knowing which was the Russians' vehicle. His only option was to sit it out and wait for them to appear.

Jackie came out fifteen minutes later and joined Andy in the Land Rover. "Those two were the Russians."

"Yup, I know," said Andy. "The girl at Reception confirmed it."

It would look odd to an observer that Andy and Jackie had been sitting separately in the dining room but were now together in the Land Rover. To deal with this Andy put on a baseball cap, a false moustache, dark glasses, removed his reversible jacket, turned it inside out and put it back on. Due to his long hair Jackie's appearance was not easy to change. Andy's appearance change was not foolproof, but he thought if seen, it was good enough to stop him being identified by a casual observer as the same man who had not known Jackie earlier at breakfast.

They didn't have long to wait. About twenty minutes later Jackie was just suggesting to Andy that he should go into the hotel to see if he could get two takeaway coffees when Yevgeny and Alexei came out. They were looking straight ahead and as they walked to their 4 Series BMW, Andy got several good side-on photographs. They left Tintagel and headed for the A39 where Alexei turned north towards Bude.

Andy had not had a chance to put a tracker on the BMW which meant that Jackie had to use all his skills to make sure the Russians didn't realise they were being followed. He was lucky that Alexei was driving quite showly, which gave him more options to keep a good distance between the two vehicles. Andy and Jackie were only too aware that they were tailing two professionals who would have been trained to spot when they were being followed.

The Russians spent all day in and around Bude and, working separately, either Andy or Jackie had eyes on for virtually the whole time. The Russians parked in the Summerleaze car park and Jackie parked several rows away on the other side. Just as Gerald's teams and Igor and Magd had done before them, the Russians walked all over the town, making sure they knew the lie of the land. They had lunch in the Brendan Arms next to the Falcon Hotel and after lunch went next door into the hotel where they had coffee in the bar.

Alexei stayed in the bar while Yevgeny explored the hotel's first and second floors, including a visit to the same outside garden which Igor had identified as his team meeting place.

Jackie had noticed his VW van parked near the Falcon in the Crescent Car Park with the MI6 VW drawn up alongside it. He knew Andy was watching the Russians in the Falcon, and from an earlier call to Gerald knew that Richard and Ox had followed Igor's whole group to Rock.

There was none of the opposition around to see him, so he approached the pair of VW vans, slid the side door of his van open and got in to find Gerald and Maddie sitting at the small fold-up table having a cup of coffee.

The MI6 van was fitted out with screens and equipment along the sides and had four swivel chairs for those working inside. In Jackie's the driver and passenger seats could be swivelled around to face the back seats and create a little sitting room with the cooker, basin and fridge on the opposite side facing the door Jackie had just used to enter.

"Well, Boss, Lady M, this is cosy. Do I get a quick cup of coffee as well?"

Jackie explained that he didn't have long because as soon as the Russians left the Falcon he would have to take over the job of tailing them from Andy.

They talked about the day so far. It had been quiet because Igor's whole group were at sea playing with their new boat which was why the MI6 team in the VW van next door and Gerald and Maddie had basically been on standby all day.

Gerald told Jackie that Richard and Ox were hanging around in Rock to get eyes on Igor's team when they came back ashore and would then follow them back to Bude. He said Maddie and he and the MI6 team would stay in Bude until Richard and Ox shepherded their Syrians back and would then return to Tiverton. He told Jackie to follow the two Russians back to Tintagel, make sure they were tucked up for the night, then put a tracker on their vehicle and head back to Tiverton.

The River Camel Estuary has the town of Padstow on one side and the small fashionable holiday village of Rock on the other. All day a ferry carries people back and forth from one side to the other. As well as being a popular holiday destination Padstow is a working fishing port with a long and proud history. During holiday times the estuary is a hive of activity with a large number of leisure and working vessels all sharing the water. A sand bar in the estuary called the Doom Bar gets its name from the large number of wrecks under the waves on the seabed. It is also home to tales of mermaids, pirates and smugglers.

Magd was the only one on board their boat who was not totally happy being at sea, his fear of being seasick always limited his enjoyment. Igor and the six Syrians were not only good sailors but most of them were skilled at handling small- and medium-sized leisure boats. After arriving at the quay in Rock the Syrians loaded diving equipment and fishing rods. They weren't expecting to use the angling equipment but needed to visibly support their cover story. They steamed down to the estuary past Polzeath beach on their right and then passed Gulland Rock which was also on their right-hand side.

All six Syrians took turns driving the boat and everyone familiarised themselves with the navigation instruments. They went north-west towards Trevose Head and did a circuit of the Quies Islands where they spotted seals sunbathing on the rocks, while other seals could be seen in the water in several places. Two of the divers, Akram and Khalifa, put their wetsuits on and swam over to the islands to snorkel with the seals and have a close look at them. Daoud put his mackerel rod over the side and in only a few minutes caught several fish which he threw to the seals before they pulled up their anchor and left.

Just before 1:00 pm the group were steaming back into the estuary, heading for their berth at the Rock Marine quay. There had been a failure in their planning for the day in that they hadn't brought anything to eat or drink with them.

After mooring the boat and loading all their gear back into their vehicles the group caught the ferry across the estuary to Padstow in search of lunch. They enquired which was the best place to eat and were referred to Rick Stein's Seafood Restaurant.

They had not made a reservation, so were told to come back in an hour in case there had been a cancellation for the second lunch sitting. Being at sea the whole morning had given them all appetites which couldn't wait an hour, so they walked back along the quay and ended up in the Basement Café and Restaurant.

There were no other plans for the day. The next day would be a long day at sea when they headed out to meet the *Annie Mae;* so Igor decided they would take the afternoon off and relax. Part of relaxing meant that even though they were Muslim, several bottles of wine were drunk.

This eliminated the normal caution the group would have had which played into the hands of Richard and Ox who were keeping them under surveillance. They had caught the next ferry and followed Igor and his men to the Padstow side of the estuary, where they continually made minor changes to their appearance and took turns to keep an eye on the group. The Old Custom House Pub is only a few yards away from the Basement Café. Richard and Ox separately had lunch there while the other stayed outside keeping watch on their targets.

It was mid-afternoon when the Syrians and Igor got up and made for the ferry to cross back to Rock. Richard and Ox couldn't risk going on the ferry because they would be too close to the group for too long. Instead of following them they called the MI6 team who were in the VW van in Bude and alerted them that Igor and his people would soon be in their cars, and so the tracking devices should show them heading back to Bude.

Later that evening at Tiverton Castle Gerald had another long conversation with Ros who was due to travel back to Tiverton the next day. Gerald admitted to her that until now he had been worried about gaps in information, lack of control, lack of options and he wasn't sure exactly how all his people would work together. He now told Ros he was much more confident, he had tracking devices on all the opposition's vehicles, listening devices in Igor and Magd's rooms, he knew where Yevgeny and Alexei were, where the *Annie Mae* lay, and his people were working really well together, having become an adaptable, effective and cohesive unit.

They discussed the meeting the next day between Igor's group and the *Annie Mae* which would happen at sea. Through binoculars boats at sea can be identified from long distances. This meant Gerald couldn't risk going to sea with Cole and Maddie to shadow Igor on his way to the meeting.

Ros volunteered to organise satellite surveillance and said she would also organise a couple of fly pasts by civilian helicopters or light fixed-wing aircraft to increase the eyes on capability.

Gerald said that because it was vital to know as much as possible about what Igor brought ashore from the *Annie Mae*, he would send the MI6 team, and Jackie and Andy separately to Rock the next day to stake out the quay area so that when Igor returned and unloaded his equipment they would have the maximum amount of chances to get all the photographs possible.

So far, apart from Magd raping and beating up a local girl,

none of Igor's group had done anything wrong or broken any laws. However, as soon as they brought ashore the weapons, explosives and other equipment to be used in their attacks they would be on the wrong side of UK law, and the evidence-gathering process could start.

He explained that Andy in one vehicle and Christine in another would follow Igor to Rock, and then, while he was at sea, they would have all day to work out where and how to position themselves to get the best photographs when Igor's group returned. Gerald told Ros he would swap people around the next day and send Richard and Ox to keep an eye on the pair of Russians in Tintagel instead of Jackie and Andy.

20

Igor steamed straight out to sea, heading for the coordinates Moscow had given him the night before. An hour out from Padstow he was in radio contact with Captain Pandelis on the *Annie Mae*, and an hour and a half after that, the two vessels had fenders out and were alongside each other.

The crates that Pandelis had been carrying for Igor were brought up on deck and opened so that Magd and his men could check out all the equipment and take what they needed for the attacks. There were no other vessels visible in the area and Igor had no reason to think he was being watched. A small light aircraft had flown over them just before they met the *Annie Mae*, but the plane had long since disappeared to the north and the only other aircraft had been a helicopter in the distance.

Caution and not taking chances had long been driving principles for Igor. He told the captain to rig up some tarpaulins as awnings so that Magd and his men could check their kit without the danger of being observed by eyes in the sky. He also instructed the captain that neither he nor his crew should take cell phone photographs of him and his men or the equipment they were looking at.

Igor wasn't to know it but it was too late. A satellite had already taken a series of photos as the two boats came together and most of those on both boats had been visible on deck at the time. A short while later another satellite had photographed items being taken out of the crates and laid on the deck. Two curious members of Pandelis's crew had also surreptiously taken images of Igor, Magd and the six Syrians on their cell phones.

The decision as to what equipment to take was made by Magd with input from the divers and anglers. They chose a selection of automatic weapons, including Iranian-made 9 mm pistols and AK47 assault rifles made in the Czech Republic.

Igor had stressed to Magd that responsibilty for the attacks would be claimed by the Islamic People's Front and the choice of equipment must back this up wherever possible. Magd chose six small Iranian-made drones which would be independently pre-programmed for six targets on the ground at the GCHQ site. Each drone would carry a payload of about 12 kgs (26.4 lbs). The high explosives chosen for both the drones to carry and the divers to place on the seabed around the cable all bore Iranian identification markings.

They selected 300 kgs (660 lbs) of high explosives which would be 72 kgs (158.4 lbs) to be carried by the anglers and 228 kgs (502.6 lbs) which would be split and laid in two places on the Google cable by the divers. Fuses, detonators, timing devices and heavy-duty carrying nets were added to the equipment taken.

Magd smiled at the irony that the Russians wanted to be able to deny responsibility, but were quite happy to help point the finger at Iran which was supposed to be a Russian ally.

A full medical kit, various tools and combat knives were also selected together with six RPGs. The equipment was wrapped in tarpaulins and loaded onto Igor's boat.

Captain Pandelis watched the selection and loading process and noted that there would be quite a lot of equipment which the Russians and the Arabs wouldn't take. Shoulder-fired missiles, RPGs, weapons, explosives and even four mortars were all not needed. The captain's imagination was in overdrive trying to think of contacts he could approach to sell the armaments to when Magd and his men started taking everything they didn't want out of the crates and dumping it over the side. The Javelin missiles had particularly caught the captain's eye, and he watched dismayed as they were among the last items to be sent to the bottom of the sea.

Once the transfer of equipment had been completed and the items either stored in lockers or hidden under tarpaulins, Igor and Magd shook hands with the captain, went back aboard their own boat and headed to the Cornish coast.

All seven of those on board with Igor, and Igor himself, shared the same feelings of excitement mixed with fear and anticipation because they all realised the operation had entered a new phase. They were no longer ordinary visitors to the UK, innocent tourists who could go home. They were now in possession of weapons and explosives, and if they were caught they would go to prison for a very long time.

On the way back to Rock Magd explained the reasons for having selected what he had. As far as possible he had chosen Iranian equipment, Magd's men thought they were working for the IPF, so that made sense to them. Magd further explained that they didn't know what invisible defensive layers there might be at GCHQ like the jamming of radio signals and wifi. This was why he had chosen the relatively simple and low-tech drones which once programmed, would fly to their targets unless shot down. All the men had participated in the selection, so there were no questions.

When Igor reached Rock and the men were tying up on the quayside they were being continually photographed by Andy, Christine and George who had chosen good vantage points while their quarry had been at sea. The explosives were left in the locked storage in the wheelhouse which itself was also locked. The other items were still wrapped in the tarpaulins when they were loaded into the boots and onto the back seats

173

of their vehicles.

Igor's plan was to go to sea again on the next day so that Magd and his men could prepare all the equipment without being seen. He didn't like the idea of driving around with the weapons and equipment in the vehicles, but he had no option because there was not enough safe storage out of sight on the boat. Neither Igor nor any of the men expected to have to use weapons; nevertheless, from now on each man would carry an automatic pistol.

In the mid-afternoon when Igor and his little convoy left Rock to return to Bude not only were they unaware they were being followed and their vehicles tracked, they were also not aware they were effectively being escorted. Ros, Gerald and the MI6 planners now had part of the proof they would need to arrest Igor and his group and play the end game as planned.

However, they only had part of the proof. The items in the boots of the vehicles proved that Igor's group were dangerous foreigners in possession of equipment which could be used to attack and destroy a variety of targets, and kill a large number of people. The proof that was missing was which actual targets they planned to attack, when and how. Photos were now being taken, Igor and Magd's hotel rooms contained listening devices, and Andy and the MI6 guys had various long-range listening devices, including lasers which were also being used to gather evidence.

Until the evidence gathering was complete MI6 did not want any unforeseen incidents upsetting the process. Whenever any of Igor's vehicles were on the move they would now be even more closely shadowed than before, and if any vehicle were in an accident or stopped by the police, MI6 would quickly intervene to keep the local police out of the picture, and throw a blanket of silence over anything that happened.

Alexei and Yevgeny had to check out and test their equipment. They needed to assemble their weapons, test them and inspect other items like the nerve agent poison which had been sent in the Russian Embassy package. They bought a large locking storage box which they left in the boot of their BMW with the kit inside. They didn't like the idea of keeping their equipment in the vehicle anymore than Igor did but they had no choice, leaving incriminating weapons in their hotel room clearly wasn't an option. After killing Igor and Magd they planned to dump their weapons and other equipment in the Tamar Lakes near Kilkhampton.

They had been keeping their eyes open for a quiet secluded place to assemble and test-fire their weapons and zero in their sniper rifle, and had decided that although there looked to be lots of open country there was nowhere which was secluded enough for a series of gunshots to go unnoticed and not be investigated. They decided to do the tests out at sea where they could wait until there were no other boats in sight, fire a few shots and then move to another location and repeat the process until they had tested everything to their satisfaction.

Richard and Ox had been parked outside the Camelot Castle Hotel since 07:00, ready to follow the assassins. They knew which car they were driving from photographs which Andy had sent to their phones. Since they arrived they had been debating going into the hotel for breakfast but decided it was too much of a risk. They would have to breakfast one at a time to avoid missing the Russians altogether if they left from the front door while Richard and Ox were in the dining room.

They weren't worried that they might lose the Russians due to the tracker on their vehicle, but as Gerald stressed time and again, "Trackers can't see, unless you have eyes on, it is always possible to miss something important, even a detail can make a difference between life and death." So they sat it out in the car park thinking about coffee and breakfast and taking occasional swigs from their water bottles.

Their patience was rewarded when the Russians appeared at 09:30 and drove off. They went from Tintagel to the A39 at Camelford and then turned south towards Padstow, Rock and the Camel Estuary. Richard and Ox varied the distance between themselves and Alexei and Yevgeny who were obviously in no hurry.

Richard called Gerald to report that their targets were on the move and asked him what was going on at the Bude end. When he heard that Igor had gone to Rock and his team had taken their boat to sea Richard commented, "Interesting, it's a little early to say but we will know in a few minutes where our boys are heading. I would think it would be Padstow or Rock. I don't see why they would go further south."

Gerald agreed. "Yup, you are probably right. Good job that Igor and his merry men are at sea or they might bump into each other, although I guess that is a one-way street, because your killer boys know who Igor and Magd are but not vice versa."

Fifteen minutes later Richard called Gerald again. "They went to Wadebridge and turned off, and are now definitely heading for Rock. What do you want us to do?"

Gerald told Richard to keep following them and pointed out that Andy and Jackie and Christine's team were already at Rock waiting for Igor's return, so they could take their holiday snaps.

"I will call Andy and Christine and tell them to let you know where they are. Depending on what your boys are up to it could get a little crowded in Rock when Igor gets back."

Minutes later Alexei turned into the car park of the Pityme Inn and he and Yevgeny went into the pub. Ox went in to use the toilet and came out and told Richard they were having coffee.

The Pityme Inn is only a very short distance from Rock Marine, and after they had finished their coffee Rock Marine turned out to be the next stop for the two Russians.

Richard and Ox had driven past the Rock Marine gate and parked so they could watch for when their targets left the boatyard. They didn't have to wait long before the Russians came out, got back into their BMW and drove to the Rock Marine quay where they parked and unloaded a large box onto a 6 metre Rock Marine self-drive RIB, before heading out into the estuary.

Gerald and Richard were in constant communication during this time and Andy and Christine had been looped in.

"Jesus, I hadn't expected this. I wonder what the hell is going on?" Andy was the first to comment to Gerald.

"It's either a coincidence or they and their large black box are heading out to meet Igor, and if that's the case, what will they do, attack and kill them? There could be a battle if Igor now has weapons on board. Or maybe there has been a change of plan we don't know about and all these bad guys are now working together?!"

Gerald replied, "I don't think so; there is something we don't know. This doesn't feel right. Christine, please get Ros to call me on my burner and we will keep this loop open. If Cole wasn't on station up off Bude he could follow the Russian pair." His burner phone came to life seconds later. "Wow, that was quick, Ros. We might have a little complication."

He updated Ros and asked if she could get a helicopter up

as soon as possible to keep a distance but keep an eye on the two Russians. Ros was soon back on the line.

"Done, my friend. We'll be overhead the killer boys in a short time. It is the same guy who has been watching Igor from afar. From where he is now, he reckons he can be back at the mouth of the estuary in 10 to 15 minutes."

There was nothing Gerald hated more than being blind. The next 17 minutes really dragged by until Ros came back to him.

"Panic over, they have turned south-west and are heading away from Igor's last position, but that doesn't answer what the hell they are up to."

A short time passed; then the pilot reported in and Ros's question was answered. The pilot had to stand off quite a distance and use powerful binoculars, which, although stabilised, still shook with the vibrations of the aircraft. He later reported that Alexei and Yevgeny had moved three times, and he was sure weapons had been fired at each place they stopped.

Gerald didn't want his people tripping over each other, so he ordered Richard and Ox to withdraw and find somewhere close to stand by. They had missed breakfast having had to sit outside the Pityme Inn while Alexei and Yegeny were inside having coffee, so now decided it was their turn and went back to the pub for something to eat. They were there when Igor's crew returned to Rock and were photographed by Andy, Christine and George, and once Igor's two vehicles were being covertly escorted back to Bude, Gerald told Richard to go back to the quay, wait for the return of the two Russians and then keep on their tail.

Alexei and Yevgeny had no way to know that Igor had bought his boat from Rock Marine and had also rented a quayside holiday berth from the same company. They had looked online for where to charter a boat for a day and the best option they found was to rent a self-drive RIB from Rock Marine for three days for £975.

They only needed the boat for one day but money was not a consideration, so they did not worry about having to pay for the two days they would not use the boat.

They took with them a bag with various objects which would float and so could be used as targets. They were lucky that there was very little wind and the sea was flat calm.

All the weapons had been sent to them stripped down; so had to be re-assembled. For the pistols and the AK47s it was just a question of putting them together and firing a couple of shots to see if they worked properly.

The sniper rifle was a different matter. Alexei was the sniper and he would have liked to zero the weapon in on a proper target, shooting from a solid unmoving fixed platform. This was not possible when shooting from a moving boat at targets which were also moving, even though the movement was very slight.

He decided to work on a head shot at 100 metres. It only took three shots for him to be hitting plastic bottles much smaller than a human head every time. They brought a couple of blankets and cushions with them, and used these to muffle the sound of their shots. The sniper rifle and the pistols had screw-on silencers and they tested the weapons both with and without those devices.

In addition to their weapons Alexei and Yevgeny had been supplied with organophosphorous compounds known as Novichok nerve agents, which, after entering the human body were almost undetectable and the damage caused was incurable. They had been provided with six small bottles, together with syringes, a walking cane and a small rigid briefcase. The

Novichok could be stabbed into the victim using the syringe in the cane, injected, put into food or drink, or the briefcase had a button which when pressed released a robust syringe which could be used in a crowd or a brush past to stab the victim.

The other items on the inventory were two stiletto knives with 9 inch blades and two wire garrottes. Clearly none of these could be left in a hotel room; so that was why they had to be checked at sea, away from eyes and ears, and then stored in the locked box in their vehicle.

They had the boat for the day and had nothing else to do, so spent the rest of the afternoon close in shore, exploring the coast around the Padstow estuary area.

Two hours after Igor and Magd had left Rock Marine to return to Bude their potential assassins tied their self-drive boat up on the same little quay close to where Igor's boat had been moored a short while before.

Richard watched them coming to shore, tying up their boat and then walking off, heading for their car. He then called Ox to come and pick him up and they followed the killers back to their hotel in Tintagel.

After an early dinner at Tiverton Castle Gerald, Ros and the whole group held a council of war. Ros had brought another surveillance van with her and two more MI6 electronics people to work inside it. The van had the same equipment as the one Christine had been using, including long-range laser-listening devices.

Gerald and Ros now had a large range of listening and surveillance capabilities, as well as Ros's Moscow source who was reporting regularly. They knew that Igor planned to be at sea the next day, and then had allowed a spare day before the attacks which were planned for the day after. Although it was Ros's money, Ros's government and mostly Ros's people, Gerald had operational command and he outlined his plan and gave his orders.

"I think, I hope, we are still ahead of the game and now the game is near the end. Tomorrow we expect Igor to go to sea on their boat for a final play with their kit. They are then keeping a day in hand before mounting their attacks on Friday. They have chartered Vincent for the day and based on what we know and can guess this is what to expect:

"The anglers will go with Vincent and mount the attack on GCHQ from his boat and will kill him either before or after the attack. No way will they keep him alive. The divers will come up from Padstow in their boat and set charges on the cable. We don't know yet where Igor and Magd will be, maybe they will stay ashore, or maybe one will go with each attack team.

"We also don't know the detail of their escape plan after the attacks, but we do know that their first step will be to head out to sea and RV with the *Annie Mae*. We will prevent the attacks and there will be no escape. We will intercept Vincent as soon as he leaves Bude, but there is still too much we don't know. Ros is moving an SBS* team to Bude tomorrow who will be bringing their own RIB and kit.

"There will also be an RAF helicopter close by and armed police waiting in Bude. Christine, you will go with George, William and Henry and follow Igor when they leave Bude and arrive in Rock. Then wait there until they get back. Pack some things; during the day one of you call a hotel or guesthouse in Bude and book in. From now until the end of the operation we will all be based in Bude.

"Keep laser listeners on them as much as possible whenever they are outside their vehicles and pick up everything you can. I am tempted to have Andy go to Bude now and put audio transmitters in their vehicles, but we can't take even the tiniest chance that they would be discovered because that would blow the whole operation and they would run.

"Richard, you and Ox go with the new guys from MI6 in their van and hang tight to our two friends in Tintagel. Don't risk getting caught but keep close and use laser listeners.

"Andy and Jackie, you go and search their rooms in the Falcon and in the Premier Inn. If you get caught, then call Ros immediately and she can square the guys in the hotel or even the local police. Also please pack some things and arrange accommodation in Bude for the next three or four nights.

"Maddie and I will be moving back to Bude tomorrow, but will stay close to our house and out of sight as much as possible so that we don't risk a chance meeting with Igor. If we need any errands run around town we will use Michelle Bolt as our messenger to lessen our visibility. OK, everyone early to bed and out of here first thing. We will all meet at our place in Bude tomorrow evening. Come in the back way and try to make sure you are seen by as few people as possible. Keep in touch, everyone, all day tomorrow. Maddie and I will be at home in the office with Michelle standing by in case we are needed for anything."

*NOTE – SBS stands for Special Boat Section which is the Royal Navy's special forces and the equivalent of the Army's SAS.

The waves breaking on Crooklets Beach in Bude under which runs the Google Transatlantic Cable.

21

On Wednesday morning Gerald and Maddie woke very early and sat on their balcony overlooking Crooklet's Beach watching the nearly flat sea sparkling as the sun reclaimed the land and the sea from the night. Bude was waking up, and slowly the beach and the grass downs came alive as dog walkers, surfers and hikers started appearing. They sat in silence, each aware that there was an extra dimension of tension in the air. In two days' time the game would reach its climax when Igor's people tried to carry out their attacks. Gerald's group didn't only have to stop the attacks, they had to do so bloodlessly, if possible, and gather evidence and confessions, before Gerald had to play his crucial role with Igor.

Ros and her agents had secured rooms in the Beach Hotel, and Andy and Jackie were in the Karenza Hotel.

All the players on both sides felt similarly when they woke and began their day. Like Gerald and Maddie, they were all aware of a new dimension of tension in the air as the potentially deadly game moved towards its climax.

The only two players who were utterly relaxed were the killers staying in the Camelot Castle Hotel in Tintagel. Alexei and Yevgeny were just waiting to do their job and go home. They weren't only professional killers, they were professional killers with no agenda, they just followed orders. They didn't think in terms of taking human lives, they thought of targets, and Igor and Magd were simply moving targets. The only feelings the two killers had that came close to emotion were boredom and frustration: boredom when they were playing the waiting game as they were doing now, and frustration when events beyond their control threatened the successful completion of a mission.

Alexei and Yevgeny liked Cornwall, and on the Wednesday before the attack they enjoyed killing time exploring various places of interest around Tintagel. Until further orders came from Moscow theirs was a waiting game.

Igor, Magd, the divers and the anglers all left Bude in three vehicles after breakfast. They were not only followed by Christine, George, Henry and William in the VW van, but they also had two special police teams behind them in two unmarked vehicles which made up a strange six-vehicle convoy in which several of the players didn't know of the existence of the others.

Ros was worried that sod's law might intervene now at the end of the game if for any reason Igor's vehicles and their contents came to the attention of the public. A road accident, the theft of a vehicle, being stopped for speeding or other unlikely but possible events, could completely derail the operation, so the unmarked two-vehicle four-man special police escort had strict orders to keep all three of Igor's vehicles under surveillance all day.

Igor's vehicles stopped briefly at the Rock Marine pontoon to unload and then parked in the car park at the end of the road where the police vehicles and Christine also parked. Christine followed the group on foot for the two minute walk back to the pontoon and then watched Igor's boat move out into the estuary, heading for the open sea.

There was no reason for Cole Benson to take up his watch station off Bude that day because all of the opposition were at sea off Padstow. Gerald had called Cole the evening before, had described Igor's boat and told him to follow it out to sea and keep loose contact with it.

Gerald would have liked Andy to accompany Cole and take photographs of whatever Igor's teams did, but even with a very long lens Andy would have needed to get so close that there would be a risk of Igor becoming suspicious. Images of Igor's activities could be obtained by the satellites, and so, although Andy's crystal clear photographs would have been desirable, they were not essential.

Cole's orders were to keep Igor just in sight and call Gerald with any position changes; also inform Gerald when Igor started heading back into Rock so that Christine and the police escort could be alerted to their imminent arrival.

Igor was not aware of Cole as he followed him out of the estuary, but two hours later when they were out at sea with no other vessels in sight he did spot Cole's RIB. Igor had seen large numbers of recreational angling boats going in and out of the estuary, so when he checked Cole out using his binoculars and saw an angler sitting with his feet up on the tube on the side of the boat, drinking from a mug he took no notice.

Cole soon drifted out of sight before repositioning. This was the strategy he followed all day. A few minutes in binocular range, then disappear, then reappear. During the day other boats came within Igor's binocular range, so Cole's on and off presence didn't arouse suspicion.

All the weapons Magd had chosen were silenced, and when they had no other boats in their vision they test-fired their weapons and reloaded them and the spare magazines. The divers unpacked their explosives and prepared them for being lowered down to the Google cable, called Grace Hopper, ready for detonation.

To cover all bases, Magd told them to ready one set of charges to be triggered by radio signal and the others by timers. They would all go off at the same time, but if for any reason one detonation method were to fail, the other would provide back up.

Daoud, Suleiman and Ahmed assessed the six drones and spent time test-flying them and studying how to preprogramme them to fly into the GCHQ dishes and explode. They had been slowly drifting north while they tested their drones and readied their other equipment.

Once this exercise had been completed they steamed at speed to Bude and briefly anchored about 500 metres off Crooklets Beach. The divers knew where the cable was but wanted to do a final position check before blowing it up on Friday.

As soon as they arrived, Khalifa and Mohammed got into their wetsuits and put on their scuba tanks before going over the side and diving down to the seabed.

It took fifteen minutes of working a search pattern to find the cable which, as expected, lay at a depth of just under 15 metres. The cable was about 8 inches in diameter, was brownish in colour and had a growth of seaweed on it.

The pair surfaced, climbed back on board, and then Akram turned south heading back towards Padstow.

At maximum binocular range Cole had been watching them all the time.

While Magd's men busied themselves with the weapons and explosives Igor studied his maps. Two days earlier he had visited the book shop in Bude and been served by Christian Single, the owner. He had bought two maps of the North Cornwall area. One was a road map and the other an Ordinance

Survey publication.

Igor was old-school, he liked to know where he was and what was around him in the general area, so that he felt properly orientated. Cell phone and tablet screens and personal computer screens were all too small for him to get the feel he wanted when familiarising himself with an area.

Single had been chatty and enquired what Igor was doing in Bude. Igor fell back on his sea angling cover. He remembered his shark-fishing trip years before with Gerald and spoke of his more recent days out with Vincent Headon.

In many years of retailing Single had served and chatted to thousands of customers. Most were instantly forgotten, some left lasting good impressions and some bad, while others found a way into his consciouness, and like an itch that couldn't be scratched, lodged in his mind question marks that often resurfaced without answers. Igor was in the last category, he was an enigma, someone Christian Single thought might be significant but didn't know why. There was no way he could have known that the man who had become a question mark in his brain planned devastating attacks only a few miles from the sleepy town where Cole Benson said nothing ever happened.

In the middle of the morning Bude's chief fire officer was at the station where he received a phone call telling him to stand by for a video call. Ten minutes later his own superior and the Chief Constable for Devon and Cornwall Police, were on his computer screen alerting him to a drill for an unspecified national emergency. He was told to park all his fire engines outside the fire station and be on hand three hours later to open the station and receive some visitors that he must not tell anyone about.

Two and a half hours after the video call two dark blue Land Rovers, one of which was towing a tarpaulin covered RIB, pulled into the Crescent Car Park and drew up alongside the two VW vans inside which Ros and Gerald were sitting out of sight waiting for them.

Introductions were brief and then Gerald climbed into one of the Land Rovers and Ros into the other. Gerald directed his driver to the fire station where a rather excited but confused fire chief was waiting to open the doors to admit the men from the Special Boat Service (SBS), their 6 metre RIB and other equipment.

The fire station would serve as the SBS headquarters for the next few days. The men set about making themselves at home and turning the building into an operations base. The large doors had glass panels in the centre which were blacked out from the inside. The tarpaulin was taken off the RIB, camp beds were set up and within 15 minutes Captain Jonathan Kerr was asking Gerald and Ros if they fancied a brew of tea.

While the men sorted out weapons and busied themselves with other kit, Gerald and Ros briefed the Captain. In special forces units rank and formality are less rigidly observed than in regular units, and all the men listened intently while the two civilians briefed their boss.

Gerald pointed out that the SBS had one RIB but there were two targets. Ros apologised if in any way her request had not been specific enough, but told the Captain she had definitely asked for two boats.

Gerald commented that he had a large RIB available, that he had considerable exposure to combat situations, having been in various war zones, had worked with MI6 for many years, and had experienced several other situations which involved the use of weapons. He explained that his friend Cole had been in the army and had ended his service in the parachute regiment.

189

He offered his boat and both his and Cole's services.

Initially the Captain said he would take Gerald's boat but neither Gerald nor Cole. Ros couldn't pull rank but she could pull influence, and she told the Captain that this was a MI6 operation, that responsibility ended with her, that neither Gerald nor Cole need be involved if there was combat. They were both experienced enough to know to keep their heads down and keep out of trouble.

Captain Kerr reluctantly agreed, having satisfied himself that he had put up enough of an argument so that if anything went wrong and either Gerald or Cole were caught in a crossfire, his men could back up that he had no choice and the decision had not been his.

Before Gerald and Ros left, a four-man armed police unit arrived, asking for Ros. This was the team Ros had requested which would conduct the arrests on the Friday after the SBS had rounded up and disarmed Igor and his men.

Ros told them to go find accommodation and be back at the fire station the next morning at 10:00 for a briefing which would be for all those involved in the Friday's operations.

For the next two nights the SBS men would sleep in the fire station and would only go out wearing civilian clothes. On Friday they would go into action wearing their combat fatigues but with no insignia or badges of rank.

Much as he enjoyed fishing Cole was getting bored by the time Igor started heading back towards the estuary. He called Gerald to inform him of Igor's return while he was at the fire station. Gerald said he would alert Christine in Rock and told Cole to follow Igor back to the estuary and be at the Bude fire station for a meeting at 10:00 the next morning.

Igor's mind was far away as Akram steered their small vessel in towards the estuary and their short-term berth on the pontoon in Rock. He was thinking of sea fishing, of a life which didn't involve weapons, lies and intrigue; of living in a Western country where his two sons could prosper in freedom, and of a friend from long ago who had taken him shark fishing off Bude.

They unloaded at the pontoon, retrieved their three vehicles and without knowing it was happening, were followed back to Bude by Christine's vehicle and the two unmarked police cars.

On the drive back Igor called Vincent Headon and reconfirmed his booking of *Mantra* for Friday's all day fishing trip.

Richard and Ox were relieved when the afternoon came to an end and Alexei and Yevgeny finished their local sightseeing and went back to the Camelot Castle Hotel. Keeping eyes on the Russians all day without being detected had been difficult and challenging. Unlike Gerald, Ros, Christine and George, neither Richard nor Ox was trained or experienced when it came to covert operations. It was to their huge credit that they had managed to keep eyes on the Russians when they had gone to Rock Marine and then again today that the assassins had not noticed them or been suspicious. The next time Richard and Ox would meet them the circumstances would be very different and potentially extremely dangerous.

That evening what Gerald thought of as the "home side" – his people and the original MI6 team – met at their house. Due to Ros's Moscow source and their own diverse surveillance operations over the last several days Gerald was now confident that they all understood what they were up against and had a very good idea of what the enemy was planning.

Before the meeting started Gerald had privately expressed serious doubts to Ros. He explained that he had felt he was in control, but now it seemed he and his people were part of a circus: The SBS were in town, there were two separate police units hanging around and the fire service was involved, too. Gerald said that left to his own devices with Maddie and his own people, plus Christine, George, William, Henry and Cole, he could have dealt with the situation without needing half an army plodding around all over Bude.

Ros explained that it was not just a question of capabilities, but just as important were jurisdictions and politics. The armed forces, in this case the SBS, were the best suited and the right people for at-sea interceptions, the police were the only people who could make arrests. The other police unit was specifically present to head off any outcomes from accidents or unforeseen events.

Gerald understood but was only half convinced and Ros secretly sympathised with his doubts.

After their private meeting Ros told everyone to park at the Crescent Car Park the next morning where the VW vans would once again serve as their mobile headquarters. The MI6 electronic watchers would remain in the vans monitoring their surveillance equipment while at intervals everyone else would make their way singly and in pairs to the fire station for the 10:00 briefing.

As a nod to Gerald's misgivings and to boost his authority, she made clear that he would do the briefing, would formulate the plans and explain their execution.

Gerald listened to Ros pandering to his ego, and smiling inwardly, thought, *You devious little cow.*

Cole Benson had listened all evening, saying nothing, and

his was the last question which was exactly the type of question that Ros did not want to hear.

"Shall I bring my shotgun on Friday?"

In perfectly timed unison Gerald, Ros and Maddie all said, "No!" but George was too late to stop himself saying, "Why not, ripping!"

Gerald closed the meeting by telling Ros that he wanted her second team to spend the next day at the Camelot Castle Hotel in Tintagel keeping an eye on the two assassins. He asked Andy to make sure the watchers had pictures of Alexei, Yevgeny and their vehicle.

It was a warm evening, and later that night Ros was sitting outside the Beach Hotel having a nightcap when Richard walked by. She saw him and suggested, "Join me, my shout?"

"Sure, beats walking around the town or watching TV."

Ros peered at him in the dim light, and while she waved at a waitress, said, "Hmm, I am not sure if that was a compliment!"

Richard smiled. "It was meant as one. Maybe it didn't come out quite as well as it might have done. I am just an uncultured wild white African, you know."

"You've known Gerald and Maddie a long time. Tell me about them. No secrets, just what you are comfortable with. When I saw his service number and went through his file I wasn't sure whether I should be in awe, fascinated or worried."

"Maybe a little of all three," Richard answered, chuckling in the near darkness. "They are special, I would trust them with my life, and I don't suppose I will ever come across anyone else like them. In many ways, they, and especially Gerald, are misfits, they don't really know where they belong, but what they do know is what is right and wrong in the world, and in their own way, they try to do what they can. They can drive you nuts, and drive themselves nuts, but let me tell you that Ox, myself, Andy, Jackie and, I am sure, Cole are not here just for the money or to be on the side of the angels, we're all here mostly for them. Gerald has an expression he calls T.I.T. which is 'think it through'. We all respond to what he tells us to do because not only does he often have the luck of the devil, but we all know that whatever he decides he will have thought it through every which way. He is a great planner. Now, what about you, how did you become a Lady James Bond?"

Neither she nor Richard had planned to go to bed together. At some point earlier when they were still on the terrace she had touched Richard's hand, she wasn't sure why she had done it, but he then lay his hand on hers. Nothing was said because nothing needed to be said. It was a natural, perhaps inevitable progression that led to them going up together to Ros's bedroom.

The only light in the room was from the street outside and this added an extra erotic level to the huge desire Richard felt as he took off her clothes. In an almost ritualistic way she then removed what he was wearing and stretched up so their mouths met in a long kiss. He put a hand on each of her buttocks and as he lifted her up she wrapped her legs around his middle.

It wasn't love, or lust it was just good adult sex, and it was a relief and a release they both needed badly. From different perspectives each of them knew how important their current assignment was. They hadn't been overtly aware of it but tension had been building for days, and now on the eve of the battle they had both welcomed a period of detachment from the impending reality.

After having made love for the second time Ros said, "Bugger, I hope this wasn't a mistake. I suppose I am now in danger of becoming part of your crazy gang. Don't you dare say anything to anyone, especially Gerald or Maddie, or I will kill you."

"And," said Richard, "You have a licence to kill, I suppose?"

Three hours later Ros blew Richard a kiss as he went out of her bedroom door and whispered, "Goodnight."

As he walked back to the Falcon Richard realised that for him the game had now subtly changed. Until now Ros had just been a bossy English spy. He never thought about her and had no feelings for her. Sex was sex, it had been good and he wasn't a teenager who thought he was falling in love. However, Ros had now become a woman to him and his natural instinct was to shield and protect women from danger.

He made a mental note to be careful not to let his instincts show because Maddie, for one, would be sure to notice. She would say nothing, but although the teasing would be subtle, it would continue until she felt she had had enough fun.

22

The tension that had been felt by both sides on Wednesday lessened on Thursday as everyone in their own way came to terms with the inevitablity of the next day's impending action.

For Alexei and Yevgeny the waiting and uncertainty were over, because the night before they had received confirmation from Moscow that the attacks would be carried out on that Friday.

Igor had told Moscow that neither he nor Magd would accompany the attack teams. They would stay ashore from where the explosions at sea would be visible and audible. As soon as Igor knew the attacks had succeeded and the hit teams were heading out to sea to meet the *Annie Mae* and make good their escape, he would report to Moscow. Then he and Magd would leave the Bude area and head for London's Heathrow airport and take the first appropriate flights.

Moscow ordered its killers to stay close to Igor and Magd and take them out as soon as they were told to do so. There was no way to know exactly what the circumstances would be at the time, but Alexei and Yevgeny were experienced professionals so the FSB control didn't suggest what method they should use to complete their mission. It was recognised that after the attacks there would be considerable chaos and a number of police and military units might soon be on the scene. This could go two ways, the confusion might give the killers an immediate opportunity, or it could make the kills more difficult. Moscow wanted Igor and Magd dead as soon as possible and preferably before they left Bude.

However, Alexei and Yevgeny were told that if immediate killings were not achievable they should follow their targets out of Bude and kill them on the road. It was stressed that under no circumstances should Igor and Magd be allowed to get anywhere near to London.

The only ones of the original players who were not present at the meeting in the fire station on Thursday morning were George, Henry and William. William and Henry stayed hidden inside their VW, watching their screens and listening to their audio devices.

Gerald had long thought that in one respect George was similar to Boris Johnson; surely he couldn't be the buffoon he pretended to be? He wasn't, and before they left their mobile HQ in the car park he told Gerald and Ros that he thought perhaps he should "just mosey around keeping an eye on what the opposition were up to, what?"

Gerald immediately agreed, and George began a period of wandering around between the Premier Inn in the Strand and the nearby Falcon Hotel. He sat on a wall eating an ice cream, read a newspaper over a coffee, watched the ducks in the canal basin and generally did what he would have described as "a ripping imitation at being an aimless tourist".

He had just sat down at a café opposite the Falcon Hotel called The Olive Tree when he saw the six Syrians walk across the front of the Falcon and go through the gate which led up to the garden on the hotel's right-hand side.

Inside the fire station Gerald had the floor and the SBS captain was silently admitting to himself that Gerald knew how to give a briefing and certainly seemed to know what he was doing.

There wasn't a lot to explain and Gerald, with occasional nods and affirmative grunts from Ros, went through the different roles that each team would play the next day. He stressed that the plans were expectations and that each team might have to act fast in response to changing or changed circumstances.

Gerald, Cole, Sergeant Hogarth and his two SBS men would all leave for Padstow early in the morning where Gerald's RIB was moored and then steam back to Bude where they would pretend to be fishing, while they waited for the divers to arrive over the position of the undersea cable off Crooklets Beach. Because Gerald and the divers were both coming up from Padstow he planned to leave at first light so he would be ahead of them and would be off to Bude well before they arrived. For many days Gerald's teams had covertly kept close to the opposition without ever arousing suspicion and Gerald didn't now want to run any risk of crowding the divers or being seen following their boat up the coast from Padstow. Once the divers had anchored over the cable, had their wetsuits on and were getting ready to go into the water Gerald, Cole and the SBS men would close in, take all the divers prisoner, secure them, take over their boat and stand off Bude and await further orders.

In the SBS RIB the captain would pursue and intercept Vincent Headon and the anglers on their way to attack GCHQ. Gerald explained that they needed the evidence of weapons and explosives, and both the anglers and the divers had to be caught red-handed. This meant the approaches had to be made at sea, and both Gerald's and the captain's RIBs would be visible on approach. This was unavoidable but was a very high-risk scenario. Gerald outlined two ways he hoped the risk could be reduced. Gerald's boat was obviously a leisure craft and the

SBS RIB had no markings, so could also pass as the same.

Gerald hoped that with everyone wearing civilian clothes, with fishing rods on obvious display, and approaching openly with lots of friendly shouting and waving they would have enough of the element of surprise on their side to enable successful bloodless interceptions. It was also important that interceptions happened before evidence was thrown over the side into the sea. If the divers or the anglers became suspicious and discarded weapons, explosives and other evidence it would be able to be retrieved but it would be a hassle best avoided if possible.

It was also vital that the interceptions be simultaneous and fast, so that one enemy team couldn't warn the other. To achieve this co-ordination Ox would be on the cliff above Compass Point to the south of Bude, watching for the arrival of the divers' boat, and then monitoring it closely as it headed for the cable. Richard would be on the cliffs above Northcott Mouth to the north of Bude monitoring *Mantra*.

Gerald explained that there was one vital timing consideration which was that the anglers would obviously kill Vincent Headon at some point. This could happen at any time, but it was probable they would want to kill him before making their attack and they might even do this shortly after leaving Bude harbour.

That the anglers had to be intercepted before they could kill Vincent dictated the timing of the interceptions. If the divers were positioned over the cable, preparing to dive when *Mantra* left the harbour, the timing would be perfect.

However, if the divers were in the area but not actually ready to dive they would have to be intercepted earlier at the same time that the SBS captain hit *Mantra* and the anglers in order to prevent Vincent being killed.

The cliff top observers to the north and south of Bude would be in radio contact with Gerald and Captain Kerr as they watched their target boats. It would be their observations which would decide the final timing of the two simultaneous interceptions.

Because they were going for broke, trying to catch the opposition red-handed with all the evidence of their intentions on board, the operation was complex, risky and so more dangerous than anyone would have liked. One small reassurance was that because the enemy wanted their attacks to happen simultaneously, both of their boats would be in near proximity at the same time.

Gerald asked if there were any questions, but before any questions were asked his cell phone came to life. George told Gerald that the Syrians had just gone into the gardens at the Falcon Hotel. He presumed it was to meet Igor and Magd. He asked Gerald to send Andy over with what he described as "some magic spook kit" to listen to what was being said. George had been in the right place at the right time, and it reinforced Gerald's belief that he wasn't the buffoon he pretended to be. The SBS men wanted to know what weapons the opposition would have, what training and whether they would be likely to put up a fight. Gerald could only answer as best he could.

The senior officer in charge of the police arrest team asked what plans there were in case there were casualties. Ros replied that two RAF helicopters would be waiting on the ground just outside Bude to deal with any emergencies, including taking any seriously wounded to hospital in Plymouth or Barnstaple. The same officer asked what the arrest and detention procedures were.

Gerald explained that they knew that Vincent would put to sea at 10:00 which was an hour before high tide. Gerald expected that all the action would be over very soon after *Mantra* left harbour, probably within an hour, but certainly two hours. The tide being in meant that after the interceptions, and once all the

Syrians had been arrested, they and their equipment could all be unloaded onto the small tidal quay in Bude harbour.

As soon as they stepped ashore the police would make the formal arrests but the prisoners would remain under SBS guard. The prisoners would initially be held in Bude police station before, still under SBS guard, they would be transferred to a specially prepared holding and interrogation building at the GCHQ camp.

Gerald waited for the obvious question and it was Ox who asked it. "And what about dear old Igor and Magd? They won't hang around sunbathing when they see all hell breaking loose in the bay and their friends being brought ashore in leg irons."

Gerald smiled. "Very poetically put, Ox. They will be Christine and George's job, and together with two plain clothes armed police officers, they will keep them in sight all morning. The officers will grab them as soon as the you-know-what hits the fan. And that brings me to Andy and Jackie. You guys will stick close to Moscow's lover boys, not too near, just close, and if they so much as blink suspiciously you call Ros.

"Those two will not be expecting to do anything until after the explosions, when they intend to take out Igor and Magd. There won't be any explosions. Instead they may hear some shooting and will then see lots of guns, police, SBS guys and people in handcuffs. Their orders will still be to kill Igor and Magd and they almost certainly will try it if an opportunity presents itself. As soon as they are ashore the captain will be in contact with you via Ros and with two of his men will round up the lover boys while the other two SBS guys stand guard duty over all the prisoners. That's it," concluded Gerald. "What could possibly go wrong? Don't tell me, just about everything! Seriously, if anyone has any bright ideas as to how to tighten up our plan and make it safer and more secure, please tell me."

Shaking his head and half smiling the young captain walked

over to Gerald thinking, *This really was a bunch of bloody lunatics.* He held Gerald's arm and took him to one side where they were joined by Ros.

"It's mad, it might just work, but we will need a lot of luck. I wish I could improve your plan, but given your need for evidence and catching them in the act, I can't see any other way to do it."

"I know," said Gerald, "I am very aware of just how dodgy it all is, but we are aiming for the stars."

Ros came in with, "Captain, if we can pull this off, it gives us a massive victory over Putin. After years of the world laughing at us since Brexit it will show we still have brains and teeth, and we are not an easy target. It really will be huge global news, and for once Britain will be on the right side of it. It could hardly be more important."

The captain looked at Ros and said, "OK, Ma'am," turned to Gerald, put his hand on his shoulder and said, "Good to be working with you, Sir. It'll work, we will make sure of it. Don't worry."

The meeting broke up and Gerald's home team headed back in ones and twos to the pair of VW vans in the Crescent Car Park where they found William and Henry listening to Igor holding his meeting at the Falcon Hotel while being overheard by one of Andy's laser devices.

Igor, Magd and their six men all sat around two tables which had been put together in the Falcon Hotel's garden. Andy arrived twelve minutes after their meeting started and the irony was not lost on him that Igor was giving his men their final briefing while only a few hundred yards away in the fire station on the other side of the canal basin Gerald was doing the same thing. He settled himself in Ox's room, set up his equipment, and immediately William and Henry were listening to and recording what was said as Igor briefed his men.

As had been the case from the start when Igor was involved conversations and meetings were in English. Igor didn't speak Arabic and the Syrians didn't speak Russian. Among themselves the Syrians spoke Arabic which George had been translating, but these conversations had produced very little of value. The valuable information had mostly come from Igor talking to Magd and Igor briefing his men.

Gerald, Ros and the captain later listened to Igor's briefing and were happy that what Igor had outlined to his men exactly confirmed what they largely knew already. It didn't require Gerald to make any planning changes to what he had detailed in his briefing. After listening to the recording of Igor's briefing, they went over all their own arrangements again and Ros added that she had arranged for two ambulances and other emergency services to be on standby.

She also reconfirmed that from 10:00 the following morning the two RAF helicopters would be on hand at GCHQ ready to take off and assist in any way that might be needed. She further explained that while the police units which were already directly involved had an idea what was happening, neither the Royal Air Force nor the emergency services knew what was really going on. They had all been told it was a training exercise in which they might be called to take part.

After Igor had finished his briefing he sent a long encrypted situation report to Moscow. The report was just an update and a confirmation of what the FSB control already knew. Nevertheless, as soon as it was received, Moscow contacted

Alexei and Yevgeny to repeat their orders and stress that they should be in Bude observing events and staying close to Igor and Magd from 09:30 the next day.

When an inevitable and dangerous event is impending the worst part is always the waiting. Gerald's teams spent the afternoon keeping up the surveillance of Igor, Magd and the Syrians, even though the game plan had been decided and it was unlikely that anything would change. Gerald and Ros didn't want any surprises which was why their targets were still watched and listened to closely.

Being kept occupied steadied nerves and helped keep up morale among Gerald's team. The SBS men spent the day wandering around Bude, having the occasional beer or coffee, playing cards and checking their weapons and equipment.

Richard often found himself watching Ros. For him she was no longer just the senior MI6 person, she was now also a lover and everything was different. He imagined her buttocks moving inside her jeans, he knew what her breasts looked like under her T-shirt, and when she left the VW van in the middle of the afternoon to visit the toilets in the Crescent Car Park, Richard just happened to be going into the toilet as she was coming out. As they passed each other and smiled, he asked, "Ten tonight for a night cap?"

Ros shook her head and replied, "No, I don't think so," before walking off.

At 10:15 that night Ros's burner cell phone rang and showed an unknown number. She clicked it on and a familiar voice said, "Special delivery, Madam, shall I bring it up?"

Ros's inital, "No!" was instantly followed by, "You don't give up, do you? Alright, the door is open."

Three minutes later Richard pushed on the door which was half an inch open. Stress, tensions and fear all needed to be released and their lovemaking was urgent, almost violent.

A while later Richard was smoking and Ros vaping as they lay side by side in the dark.

"I am terrified," confessed Ros.

Richard pushed some hair out of her face and tried to reassure her. "It will be fine, you have done all you can. We have a great bunch of guys on our side. They don't call me Lord Luck without good reason. Actually, I have never been called Lord Luck but I am lucky."

She replied, "It is not so much the danger that scares me, it is that it might all fail. This is a huge deal, not just for me and the Service but for the country. That is what is frightening me."

"I told you it will be fine, but if I am wrong I will never call you in the night again to make a special delivery."

Ros was no longer in lover mode, but was back in her MI6 personna. "Then you had better not be bloody wrong, had you?"

To Richard it didn't sound like a statement or a question, it almost sounded like an order.

PART FOUR

The End Game

23

A t 06:00 on Friday morning Gerald and Maddie drove to the fire station where Cole Benson was already parked and waiting. Five minutes later with Maddie driving, Gerald beside her, Sergeant Hogarth behind them and three long black holdall bags in the Range Rover's rear compartment they were on their way to Padstow. Cole was following with the other two SBS men, Jim Sweeney and Tod Pollard, in his rather elderly Nissan Patrol.

Cole sometimes missed his days in the army in the parachute regiment. Apart from the action he missed the comradeship and the banter between soldiers. As he drove down the A39 towards Padstow in his head he was back in the paras.

Tod was quiet and spent most of his time staring out of the window while Jim and Cole were busy taking the mickey out of each other. Cole had been theorising that life in the SBS was really just pleasure boating, while Jim said that in his opinion only mentally retarded people jumped out of aeroplanes.

The group were in two vehicles because not only were Cole and the SBS men large, but like Gerald, they would not be returning to Padstow that evening; so there was no point in leaving two vehicles there. Cole, on the other hand, would need his Nissan in Padstow because he would be taking the RIB back there after the action. There was hardly any traffic, so it was a fast trip, and just before 07:00 four men were going down the iron ladder to Gerald's RIB. Gerald and Maddie were on the quay above saying goodbye.

"I hate these times when you are going into dangerous situations and I am not there, it really frightens me."

With a clenched fist she emphasised her words by gently pounding Gerald's chest.

"I will be careful, and anyway, what could possibly go wrong with Cole and our three special forces guys looking after me?"

Maddie didn't answer, she cupped Gerald's face in her hands, stood on tiptoe and gave him a kiss before turning, walking to her vehicle and driving away without a backward glance.

Gerald climbed down the ladder, and as he did so, Cole's voice rose up to him, "C'mon, Boss, no time for romance, daylight's wasting."

Cole chuckled at his own wit, happy that once again he had found a use for one of the lines from his favourite film, *Jaws*. Minutes later they were motoring out of the estuary towards the sea with Rock on their right.

Hogarth looked at Gerald and said, "Surprised you let this idiot drive your boat, Boss, if it was me I wouldn't let him drive a tricycle."

The banter continued for ten minutes and then all five men fell silent absorbed in their own thoughts as Cole sped up the coast towards Bude doing a steady fifteen knots.

Just before she reached Camelford on the drive back to Bude Maddie saw a familiar vehicle heading towards her on a straight piece of road. Her dark glasses were resting on top of her head; she put them over her eyes, pulled her baseball cap lower and turned her head slightly as the three Syrians drove past her on the other side. The timing was working out well, she thought, but it was good that Gerald and the guys had left as early as they had.

Fifty-five minutes later back at her home in Bude she made a coffee which she took out to her balcony where she sat and looked at a flat calm peaceful sea. She didn't know what the forecast was but the weather looked settled, so she expected the sea to stay calm. She hadn't offered a prayer for years but she did now. She prayed that the day would be as peaceful as possible and that everyone, her people and the others, would still be alive at the end of it.

Ros, Christine, William, Henry and George all met for breakfast at the Beach Hotel at 08:00. It was already warm and Ros had arranged breakfast at the front of the hotel on the terrace overlooking Summerleaze Beach. She hadn't invited her two latest MI6 arrivals, they were in their VW van, monitoring all the electronic surveillance equipment.

They ate in silence; George had nothing to say. On the one hand, they were all relieved not to have to listen to George's Bertie Wooster utterances, but, strangely, now that he was quiet they missed having him to laugh at or get annoyed with.

Ros broke the silence. "This place is like a fucking graveyard." She turned to Christine and George and asked, "Are you two kids sleeping together?"

Christine exploded with, "What? You must be completely crazy! Him?"

George looked startled and rather worried; William slapped the table, a glass fell off and shattered, and Henry burst out laughing uncontrollably and was soon joined in his giggles by William who had stopped assaulting the table.

Beaming, Ros looked at each of her four people in turn. "Well, I didn't think the question would have quite that effect, but it worked and you lot have all woken up. Now, stop all looking as if you are going to get shot. Maybe it won't happen. Get your kit, everyone, and meet at the vans in the car park at

09:30. George, nip along to Sainsbury's and get three red, three white and three rosé; drop it all into those guys at the Tourist Information Centre and tell them the filming is still going well. They must be getting curious what we are up to, and they have probably drunk all the last lot by now. C'mon kids, chop-chop, we are not on fucking holiday, you know."

With that she got up and went up to her room to get her things. She noticed two of Richard's cigarette ends by the basin in her bathroom. He was very good usually and put them under water in the basin to put them out and then took them with him. She felt a little like a naughty school girl as she picked the dog ends up and noticed a red sign on the wall saying, "No Smoking."

Richard, Ox, Andy and Jackie had arranged to meet at the Crooklets Café for breakfast. Over the preceding weeks they had become a tight little unit and had developed both liking and respect for each other. Initially Richard and Ox had sometimes wondered if Andy and Jackie's continual mutual sniping was genuine. Now they not only realised it wasn't geniune, but often joined in the game themselves.

They had been talking about diving and surfing when Jackie suddenly changed the subject with a question to Andy. "Lady M gave me a 9 mm Sig, what did she give you?"

"A Glock," answered Andy.

Richard looked at them both and said, "So, we are all carrying weapons. If this one goes wrong it might get a little hairy. Let's hope we don't have to use them."

"I will second that," contributed Ox and they went back to talking about diving.

Not long afterwards, walking in two pairs, they were ambling up the slight hill from Crooklets into Bude town on their way to the Crescent Car Park. Gerald was at sea with Cole and the SBS men, so they reported to Ros.

She gave Richard and Ox a pair of powerful binoculars each, a camera with a long zoom lens and a hand-held radio. She finished with, "We know how we want this to go but we can't be sure how it will actually go. Just please remember that the use of firearms must be a last resort. OK, boys, head for your observation posts on the cliff tops."

The two men left the van and on the way out Richard winked at Ros who responded with a furious cold stare.

Next she dispatched Christine and George to keep eyes on Igor and Magd. "Work separately with only one of you visible at any one time. If Igor and Magd split up, then you split and watch them separately. They are still in the hotel, so position yourselves to tag them when they appear. Christine, I know that Maddie lent you a pistol. Same rule, last resort, and self-defence. Don't forget you are not supposed to be armed at all, so if you do have to use your weapon we will have to do some quick thinking and have a bloody good explanation to cover you. Off you go, maybe one of you to the hotel or the Brendan for a coffee and the other to the Olive Tree."

Seven people in the back of the VW had been rather a tight crowd and now only Handy Andy, Jackie Stewart and Ros were left. She spoke. "You know, when Gerald first told me that he wanted to hire and work with two guys called Handy Andy and Jackie Stewart I thought he was having me on, but I am really glad he brought you two on board. You have done very well and it has been great working with you. Richard and Ox are off to sit on the cliffs and sunbathe, and Christine and George should only have to watch and call me if there are problems, and because Igor is our prime target I will be watching him as well.

"But you two have drawn the short straws. The two Russians are killers, that is all they are; they would put a bullet in your heads without thinking twice. They may already be here, but if not, they should arrive any minute. Like us, they will stay close to Igor and Magd, so they can take them out when that time comes. They will know of Igor's plans; so they will be hanging around this part of town keeping an eye on him. They may stay together or they may separate.

"I am not going to tell you what to do, you are good operators and will be working, reacting to circumstances. Be careful, keep your distance, I would rather you lose them for a few minutes than crowd them in any way and blow it. They won't make their move until they know that the attacks have either succeeded or failed. This means there is a good chance that the SBS boys will be back ashore before our lover boys make their moves.

"Whatever happens, as soon as the boats are heading in, then us three, plus Christine, George, Richard and Ox must all be in the canal and harbour area. We must keep in constant touch using our radio mics. If circumstances allow, we will wait for the SBS guys and they can take out the lover boys, but if not, leave it to me and my armed police. There will be a lot fewer questions if our guns have to go off than if you guys start shooting. It will be crowded and messy out there today, and the key will be to all keep in constant communication all the time. Off you go, guys, I will be close all the time, either here, on the cliffs or around the canal basin. If any of us spot your two guys we will tell you to make sure you are on them. Good luck, see you later."

Andy walked along the Strand, heading for the centre of town so he could keep an eye on Queen Street, Belle Vue and the Triangle area, while Jackie sauntered along Breakwater Road towards the lock gates. Out at sea Jackie could just make out the dark shape of the SBS RIB towards Northcott Mouth.

The captain and his men had gone to sea early, because although they were posing as tourists on a fishing trip, he believed that to trained eyes policemen and soldiers often stood out like sore thumbs. For this reason he had wanted to launch his boat and be clear of the area before Igor and Magd, and Alexei and Yevgeny started wandering around.

At the stern of the RIB there was a rack with five long fishing rods in it, a Scottish flag fluttered from a mast and the captain had pasted a large picture of a mermaid showing very obvious naked breasts on the front of his cockpit. It was all about buying those few seconds of time which would give him the edge due to having the element of surprise on his side.

Out at sea Jackie could see the SBS boat and he knew that to his left on the cliff top Ox was in position with his binoculars. He walked past George sitting outside the Brendon Arms having a coffee, and had noted Christine on the other side of the canal basin at the Olive Tree. As well as the players he had noticed, he knew that Igor and Magd were still in their hotel and Richard was on a cliff top to the north. It was crowded indeed and now all he needed to complete the picture were the two Russian killers.

On his way back up Breakwater Road the three Syrians passed him driving the other way towards the harbour. Jackie turned and followed them, they drove onto the beach at the bottom of a stone ramp and unloaded five large black holdalls which they carried over to where Vincent Headon was waiting with *Mantra*, tied up alongside the harbour wall.

Vincent had left his vehicle parked along the wall of the ramp, but he told Dauod to reverse, go park in Breakwater Road and walk back. While Vincent, Suleiman and Ahmed waited for Daoud they chatted. Vincent's eyes kept returning to the five holdall bags. For some reason he didn't ask what was in the bags. Maybe he suspected he would be lied to, or maybe he just didn't want to know. He was getting paid way over normal rates by the Arabs and didn't want to rock the boat.

Nevertheless Suleiman and Ahmed noticed his questioning

glances and had already decided to kill him as soon as they were at sea and out of sight.

A few minutes later Daoud was back, jumped aboard and Vincent untied his lines to cast off.

Jackie watched, felt his stomach tighten and thought, the game is now on. He retraced his steps and hadn't gone thirty yards when his ear-piece came alive.

Ox's voice was crystal clear. "The party is on, folks. I can see Gerald and Cole close in shore coming up slowly from the Widemouth direction in the south, and much further out and way behind, our diver friends are moving in fast. Acknowledge, please."

"Copy," said Richard. "I can see *Mantra* heading slowly out, looks like Vincent is handing out mackerel rods."

"We're on it," added George. "Igor and his friend are walking over the bridge towards Christine at the café on the other side."

"Copy that," said Christine.

Ros came in with, "Yes, things are getting busy. Our two lover boys have just parked about 40 yards away from where I am in the car park. Andy and Jackie, head back this way, please, and get eyes on ASAP."

It was 10:00 and Bude was fully awake. Ninety-nine point nine percent of people woke and went about their business as if it was a normal day, but a handful of locals noticed tell-tale signs that something abnormal was happening.

Ron Berry was a well-known Bude character. He had been a publican, a hotelier and a nightclub owner. He was wearing a pair of orange-tinted sunglasses pushed up onto his white hair because one of the lenses was missing. He was walking across the bridge at the Falcon when he passed a woman, which was

Ros, apparently talking to herself. Two hundred yards farther on, on Breakwater Road, Jackie was coming towards him also talking to himself. One of Ron's two Jack Russell terriers tried to say hello to Jackie as he passed but Ron jerked him away and walked on. Something was going on, and it was probably a good idea to keep out of it.

Outside her house overlooking Crooklets Beach, Jill English was looking through her binoculars at a large black RIB. She had been watching the surfers on the beach when she picked up the RIB and spotted what looked like a small naked woman standing in front of the cockpit. She then realised she was looking at a mermaid. She scanned around and saw Vincent Headon's boat, *Mantra,* at the end of the breakwater heading out into the bay. Then she saw another boat heading in towards Crooklets from much farther out. It wasn't odd to see boats off Bude, but she could recognise most of the local craft and she was sure two of those she could see weren't local. She went in, made tea and brought it out to drink while she continued to watch. She had a funny feeling that something extraordinary was going to happen.

Cole came very slowly past the Barrel Rock at the end of the Bude breakwater. Gerald could see Vincent's boat ahead of him, heading north with the SBS RIB in its path a few hundred yards in front of him. Out at sea, still perhaps two kilometres away, the divers boat had turned slightly and was now heading at speed for Crooklets Beach.

Standing next to Cole, Gerald was giving instructions. "Just keep chugging forward slowly. The divers are closing in and in a few minutes Vincent will pass the SBS guys. When you see the captain start moving towards Vincent's boat you've got to close the remaining gap and we will hit the divers."

The earlier banter and jocularity had gone; the three SBS men on Gerald's boat were busy with weapons, handcuffs and other kit.

As he steered slowly towards the divers, Cole's face had become a mask of stone and Gerald's eyes were everywhere as he prayed the timing of the interceptions would come right.

Ros was on the cliff top above the Bude seapool, looking through binoculars and talking to Gerald and the captain with all the others listening. Maddie also had binoculars, and having been watching from near where Ros stood, she moved to stand beside her.

"Gerald, Captain, all good as you can see, you are closing for your interception. Captain, you get to *Mantra* first to stop those bastards killing the skipper." "That's right," came in Gerald, "I am watching them, first the captain must secure Vincent's boat and make him safe; then immediately afterwards I will approach our target. If our guys run, then no worries. I will chase them. Once Vincent is safe and *Mantra* secured we are more than halfway there."

On board *Mantra* Vincent was worried and sweating. He was suspicious and the three Syrians had picked up his nervousness. They had passed Wrangle Point, heading north when Daoud produced a handgun with silencer and pointed it at him.

"Just stay calm, my friend, nothing will happen, keep going to the big dishes up there."

Richard's voice was in everyone's ears. "Gun, I can see a gun; one of the Arabs is holding a pistol on the skipper."

The captain was next. "I am going in, that guy is only a trigger pull away from being dead."

"Yup, go, go, go!" said Gerald. "Approach slowly and lots of friendly waving if he puts the gun away. Then when you are alongside, take them. If he looks like shooting Vincent, then kill him and go in shooting."

"Roger that."

With that the captain said to one of his men, "Slow ahead, go straight for that boat, everyone look happy, lots of smiling, laughing and waving but be ready to take out any of the Arabs that produces a visible weapon."

There was silence for a few seconds as the RIB closed in, then Richard's voice "He's jumped, the silly fucker has jumped."

There was one muted cough as Daoud shot at Vincent who was in the water struggling to swim away. Ahmed was at the helm, he left Vincent in the water, turned *Mantra,* and under full throttle headed for the GCHQ dishes.

The captain's voice came back on. "That makes life much easier, the skipper is out of the equation now. They shot at him, but I couldn't see if he has been hit, I don't think so."

"Orders?" asked the SBS captain.

Gerald responded. "Pick up the man in the water, then go after your targets. The gloves are off now, go get them and bring them back. If they start chucking things into the sea try to stop them. Warning shots, shouting, whatever you like."

"Roger," said the captain and Richard watching from the cliff was heard muttering, "Good hunting."

Vincent had been shot. He was lucky no veins, arteries, bones, or organs had been hit. The 9 mm bullet had ploughed across the flesh on the outside of his upper left arm. He could see blood in the water and immediately and illogically thought, *Sharks!* Then the pain blotted out further thought as he struggled, fully clothed to look around him. He hadn't heard the SBS RIB approach and suddenly it was alongside him; two pairs of powerful arms hoisted him on board and lay him on the deck where a mermaid grinned down at him.

The captain gave a reassuring smile, "You just lie there, Sir, the lads will sort you out." He turned to his men. "Patch him up, lads. Clothes off, towels and blankets and some water, then to work." To Vincent he said, "Don't' worry, Sir, we'll go get your boat back for you. Just lie on the deck out of sight under the tube."

Seconds later, at full throttle, the SBS team was chasing after the *Mantra* and the anglers.

When Vincent hit the water the anglers knew what to do and gunned the engines, making straight for the dishes on the cliff tops that were their targets. The divers were watching the anglers' boat through binoculars, and when they realised there was a problem, they lost vital seconds having a hurried discussion as to what to do.

Gerald was closing on them fast but there was still about 400 yards between them; the divers decided to head for the GPS mark where they had found the undersea cable, drop their explosives and then run out to sea as fast as possible. They would set the timers on one lot and hope they would land on or near to the cable, and as planned would try to detonate the second lot using radio waves. Akram steered for the mark while Mohammed and Khalifa desperately tried to prepare the explosives, ready for dropping before Gerald reached them.

SBS Sergeant Paul Hogarth was struggling to watch the divers through binoculars as Cole raced towards the divers' boat. He shouted above the engine noise to Gerald. "Boat is moving too much. Sorry, Sir, but I can't see a fucking thing."

Gerald spoke to Ox watching from the cliffs. "Ox, can you see what our friends are doing?"

"Not great," he replied. "They are now quite a way from me, but I would say they are getting their explosives ready to chuck over the side."

"Cheers, Ox, Roger that." Gerald shouted to the sergeant over the engine noise, "Ox thinks our jokers are going to chuck their explosives over and hope for the best. We need to stop this, we can't gamble that they might get lucky. Fire over their heads to distract them. We'll be on them in less than a minute."

Paul Hogarth didn't need the order repeated. "Jim, a burst over their heads and Tod, a burst into the water in front of them."

As they drew near Gerald was shouting into a loud hailer, "Hands in the air, hands in the air."

It seemed to have worked because Akram put his engine into neutral and their boat slowed and stopped with Khalifa and Mohammed standing in the stern outside the wheelhouse with their hands in the air. Seconds later they were covered by Tod and Jim's automatic carbines. Cole put his engine into neutral and the two boats came together.

Gerald was keen not just to secure the Syrians but also to neutralise their explosives. He was about to issue orders when suddenly there were two sharp explosions followed by a scream, and the upper part of the wheelhouse was half destroyed.

Gerald and the three SBS men whipped around, searching for where the attack was coming from. What they saw was Cole standing only a few feet away holding his double-barrelled shotgun.

"I saw that bastard duck down in the wheelhouse holding a weapon and about to fire at us." Cole was referring to Akram who was now lying on the floor of the wheelhouse and losing a lot of blood.

"Good man, Cole, now let's tie the boats together and get this mess sorted out," said Gerald.

"I had to shoot him before he got us," explained Cole. Paul Hogarth further reassurred him with, "Well, at least you hit him, not bad for a civilian."

"Why don't you just bugger off," from Cole as he finished tying the boats together and Tod, Jim and Sergeant Paul Hogarth jumped aboard the divers' vessel.

In less than five minutes Mohammed and Khalifa were securely tied and all their weapons collected, the explosives secured and Gerald and Sergeant Hogarth were tending to Akram. One of Cole's shots had lacerated the right hand side of his face and removed part of his ear as well as hitting the side of the wheelhouse; the other blast had made a real mess of his right upper arm and chest.

"Sergeant, head in slowly, and you guys do what you can to stop the bleeding and sort his wounds out on the way."

They untied the boats and Cole slowly led the way back towards Bude with the sergeant following, driving the divers' boat, while Tod worked on Akram and Jim Sweeney pointed his carbine at the other Syrians.

Gerald and Tod worked fast. They swabbed Akram's wounds, bound him up and gave him a couple of intramuscular shots of morphine.

Gerald got back in communication. "Ros, Ox, everyone, we are done and heading back in. Captain, shout if you need back up and we will drop our captives and head back out to you."

Captain Kerr didn't respond, instead from his cliff-top observation position Richard's voice came through. "The captain is nearly on them, I will keep you posted."

Peter Vicko is one of Bude's well-known characters. He had been standing outside the Surf Life Saving Club on Crooklet's Beach when, like several others ashore, he heard shots and the two blasts when Cole fired his shotgun. His eyes went straight to where his brain had fixed the shots as coming from and he saw the two boats tied together.

"I'll check this out," he muttered to himself as he crossed the bridge over a small stream and started walking up the slope towards the path which would take him to the cliff above the Bude Sea Pool from where he knew he would be able to get a good view of the boats.

Ron Berry, Jill England and Pete Vicko had lived all their lives in Bude. Over the years they had acquired many tales to tell, but for all three of them the other stories would pale into insignificance when for the rest of their lives, they told the story of the day of the Russian attack on Bude.

24

The sound of gunfire is never mistaken by those who have heard it before, and over water sound is slightly amplified and travels fast. When Gerald's RIB closed on the divers and Jim and Tod fired their warning bursts all the players in the game heard the shots and reacted.

The anglers were speeding towards a position from where they could use their drones to attack the GCHQ satellite dishes; they watched as the SBS RIB sped after them across the flat water. They could see that the divers had been intecepted by Gerald but didn't know whether they had already dropped their explosives or not.

Ahmed was the strongest character of the three and he was at the helm with Daoud and Suleiman standing beside him as they raced toward their target.

They had a brief discussion, shouting to make themselves heard above the sound of the roaring engine. The question was, should they give up on their target, go flatout heading offshore, try to outrun their pursuers, reach the *Annie Mae* and escape, or should they fight and try to complete their mission?

They agreed on the second option and made the decision just as they reached the position from where they planned to launch their drones. They had two Kalashnikov 7.62 mm assault rifles, a Veresk submachine gun, three pistols and RPG shoulder-fired rocket launchers. They crouched in the rear area of *Mantra*, peering over the side of the boat, watching the RIB approach. Ahmed held the RPG and Suleiman and Daoud waited with the Kalashnikovs.

They knew the side of their boat would not protect them against bursts of incoming fire, but hoped by hiding they would mask their intentions. They planned to wait until the RIB was about fifty yards away and then all stand up together and open fire. The RPG and the two automatic weapons were more than capable of destroying the approaching RIB and killing all those on board.

The Special Boat Service (SBS) draws most of its recruits from the Royal Marines and is the British Royal Navy's equivalent to the British SAS or the United State's SEALS. The selection procedures are rigorous, as is the special forces training that follows.

Captain Jonathan Kerr was an experienced officer who had seen action in several places which had involved fighting in a number of different situations. His two men were similarly experienced and as soon as Vincent had received his emergency treatment the two men had prepared weapons while their captain had concentrated on the chase. One of the men was crouched behind a light machine gun (LMG) which they had quickly mounted in the bow of the RIB as the captain zigzagged towards *Mantra*.

When only about ninety yards separated the two craft the captain shouted, "We go first, can't see them, not sure what they are up to. Now, now, fire now!" and to Vincent he yelled, "Keep down, Sir, head down!"

The light machine gun opened up as the captain's zigzagging became a straight line approach. The 5.56 mm rounds easily went through the side of *Mantra*; the rear of the boat became a killing ground as the deadly little bullets buzzed around like angry hornets. Daoud took a bullet in each leg, one was a direct hit which passed clearly through his calf muscle and the other was a ricochet which hit his thigh and gouged a messy path until it struck his femur and shattered it. A tumbling ricochet hit Suleiman in the throat a split second before he was also hit in the heart. He died instantly.

Suddenly, near the rear of *Mantra* two hands appeared being held straight up in the air. One of the hands held a Kalashnikov which was tossed into the sea.

"Ceasefire, ceasefire, stop!" yelled the captain as Ahmed stood up with his hands stretched above his head. The boats came together and, with the LMG still covering Ahmed, the boats were secured alongside each other. The rear deck of *Mantra* was full of blood, and when Captain Kerr leapt into the boat he lost his footing and skidded across the deck to the other side.

"Jesus, blood everywhere," he muttered, and then louder, "Come over, careful, the floor is swimming in claret."

One of the SBS men kept the LMG trained on Ahmed, while the other jumped into *Mantra* to join the captain. Ahmed was securely bound and a hood placed over his head before he was roughly sat down in the wheelhouse and gaffer-taped to a seat.

All the weapons were collected and transferred to the RIB and Suleiman's body was wrapped in a tarpaulin. The SBS men sprinkled wound powder onto Daoud's leg wounds and injected morphine before applying tourniquets and pressure bandages. He was then bound, hooded, and taped into the seat in the wheelhouse next to Ahmed.

The SBS man who had been working with the captain gave Ahmed a couple of gentle little slaps on one cheek and asked, "How are you feeling, mate? You don't look too good. No worries. I reckon you'll have years to recover in prison. Now sit still and don't either of you do anything naughty."

Captain Jonathan Kerr was talking into his microphone. "All

224

secure. *Mantra* is secure, the skipper is still fine, one competitor fine, one injured and one gone to sleep. Orders?"

All those involved were listening and Ros and Gerald responded at the same time. Ros was ashore and had a more complete picture, so Gerald let her answer.

"Get back here ASAP, Captain. The shooting has been heard, there is considerable interest ashore, I need you here soonest. Over and out."

"Roger that," said Kerr and then he turned to his men and gave his own orders. "I'll drive our boat back, you two follow in this one. One of you drive and the other keep our guests covered, let's go."

Gerald's RIB and the captured boat were coming into Bude harbour and were only one hundred yards away from Barrel Rock when he heard Ros's exchange with the captain.

When the captain had signed off Gerald came back in. "Ros, I am coming in now, we will be at the quayside in a few minutes. Please meet me and have the police and an ambulance there. Sounds like the captain will need more police and another ambulance. Richard, Ox, your sightseeing is over. Meet me at the quay ASAP."

A few minutes later both boats were tied up on the short quay and Gerald was conferring with Ros while Cole and his two SBS companions were handing the captives over to the police and the ambulance service and unloading their equipment.

George's often rather bored and languid tones were now anything but when his voice came out of the ear pieces of all those in the group. "Igor and Magic have just gone into the Falcon Hotel almost running. I reckon they know they have lost and are grabbing their passports and will leg it."

"I am sure you are right," agreed Gerald. "Everyone except Andy and Jackie, over to the hotel fast. We are also heading there. Run, don't let them leave."

Ros, two armed police officers and he were running from the harbour to the hotel as he spoke. Still running he continued, "Andy, Jackie where are you and where are your lover boys?"

Andy answered. "We are behind them, Boss. They are walking slowly your way across Summerleaze Beach, strolling along without a care in the world."

"OK, thanks, keep on them. Richard, go find Andy and Jackie; then the three of you keep a loose net around the lover boys. Don't lose them and be careful, they will be armed and are very dangerous; so don't do anything to spook them."

Richard grunted, "Roger that" as he continued running fast back over the Downs to the action area. That he was able to cover the ground quickly and without stopping was thanks to his having kept up with jogging ever since he had retired from competitive running.

25

With everyone operating in such a small area it was only minutes before Gerald, Ros, Christine, George and Ox were outside the front of the Falcon Hotel.

Maddie had been on the other side of the canal basin and had seen all of her group converging on the hotel; so she walked over to join them.

Gerald sent Christine, George and one of Ros's two armed police up the lane to the right of the hotel and around the back of the building to close that escape route. When Gerald gave the order the policeman looked at Ros for confirmation and she nodded her assent. They ran off and soon George and the two others with guns had the back of the hotel sealed off.

Gerald suggested that Ros and the other policeman go inside the hotel and arrest Igor and Magd while Maddie and he kept an eye on the front in case they slipped past Ros.

Gerald and Maddie heard an explosion from down the canal towards the sea. Ox, Ros, Christine and George also heard it but for them it wasn't as loud. Because Igor and Magd were their prime targets they all stayed where they were and didn't go to investigate.

The captain and his men were unloading the dead Syrian, their two live captives and the weapons and equipment when they also heard the explosion. As requested they had been met by the police and an ambulance.

"Fuck! What now? We should check that out," said the captain to anyone who was listening.

A police sergeant answered, "You go, mate, we'll take this lot to join their friends at Bude police station."

The SBS men ran up the stone ramp from the little harbour to Breakwater Road. They looked across the canal to where there was a large cream coloured barge. There was total confusion; people were screaming and scrambling to get off the barge which had grey-white smoke billowing from its doors and windows.

As the SBS men ran forward with their automatic pistols in their hands they could see Richard, Andy and Jackie ahead of them apparently searching among the confused mass of people on the quayside next to The Barge Restaurant.

Ros's police sergeant stayed at the foot of the stairs while she and Ox went up to find Igor and Magd's rooms. Ox was staying in the hotel, so knew where all the rooms were which is why he now accompanied Ros rather than the police officer.

Loud persistent knocking and shouts of, "Police! Open up!" produced no result. They seemed to have gone. There was only one main staircase and that had a policeman at the bottom of it. Neither Ros nor Ox had heard a sound from that direction. They weren't in their rooms and hadn't gone down the stairs.

Ox suddenly realised that apart from the back of the hotel which was guarded, there was a third exit possibility. "The gardens!" he yelled, already running away from Ros, heading for the gardens which had another exit from the front of the hotel onto the road.

As they crossed Summerleaze Beach heading for the canal basin, Alexei and Yevgeny were continually, but almost imperceptibly, quickening their pace. Richard, Andy and Jackie had been slightly lulled by the apparently unhurried stroll of the two Russians, until suddenly they realised that the gap between them had widened considerably.

The Russians went up the stone steps by the canal lock gates and were now walking much faster inland along the side of the canal. Richard, Andy and Jackie realised that the Russians had known they were being followed and had bided their time before acting evasively and quickening their pace.

They realised there was no longer any need to maintain the loose spread-out surveillance strategy they had been using. They all ran for the little bridge across the river by the side of the beach. They met at the bridge and sprinted to the stone steps which would take them up to the canal lock gates. As they ran, there were two very loud bangs.

They reached the top, looked left and one hundred yards up the canal towards the main basin they saw total chaos. Smoke was coming from a large cream coloured barge which had been converted into a restaurant. People were staggering off the barge holding their heads. Two people fell off the gangway and collapsed onto the quayside.

"Fuck, Gerald will kill us, let's see if those bastard Russians are still there," shouted Richard as they ran towards the confusion. They were there in seconds and Richard started searching the barge pushing between dazed and frightened people, while Andy and Jackie checked everyone on the quayside. Valuable time was being lost and Alexei and Yevgeny had disappeared.

They were joined by Captain Kerr and his two SBS men. "What's happened?" asked the captain.

"Dunno," answered Richard, "The two Russian lover boys, we reckon. Probably chucked a flashbang smoke grenade in to create a diversion."

"Where are they now?" asked the captain.

Again Richard answered with, "Dunno, but we had better bloody find them."

"OK, two teams of three, they can't have gone far, let's find them," ordered the captain.

Alexei and Yevgeny realised that they would need confusion and a diversion which would attract the attention of the police and any other security officials in the area. They had to find their targets and would have more chance of finding them and killing them if the attention of the police was diverted elsewhere. As Alexei and Yevgeny approached The Barge Restaurant, Yevgeny threw a flashbang stun grenade through the door into the eating place, immediately followed by a smoke tear gas grenade lobbed in by Alexei. Then having caused their diversion the two Russian killers ran on.

Alexei ducked into a small yard by an angling shop and took his rucksack from his shoulder. Yevgeny ran on into the car park to get their vehicle.

Alexei put his hands into his rucksack and working by touch, he screwed a silencer onto the barrel of a rifle, with his back to any onlookers he took the weapon out of the rucksack and pulled the telescopic stock out to its full length. He then slid the weapon back into the rucksack. He stood leaning against the wall by the Olive Tree, watching the front of the Falcon Hotel with only the end of the rifle stock visible.

Yevgeny drove their vehicle back to the quayside and parked about thirty yards from where he could see Alexei standing waiting.

Followed by Ros, Ox charged through the garden door in time to see Magd, carrying a small bag, go through the little gate leading from the gardens to the street. At the top of his voice he yelled at Magd, "Stop, stop or I'll shoot!"

His shout alerted Gerald and Maddie who were still waiting at the front of the hotel. Now they ran towards the garden exit onto the road. They saw Igor appear, followed by Magd. Both men were carrying small bags.

Igor had not recognised Gerald and he ran straight towards him heading for their car which was parked immediately to the left of the main steps leading to the Falcon hotel.

Suddenly Igor cried out, stumbled and fell when Alexei's high velocity bullet hit his thigh and the rear glass window of the car they had been running past shattered, then there was a metallic thud as a hole appeared in the boot of the same vehicle.

Gerald pushed Maddie to the ground and shouted, "Someone is shooting, get down."

Two of Alexei's shots had missed and the third had failed to kill. He ran towards Yevgeny who was already driving very slowly towards him along the quay. He threw his rucksack and rifle into the vehicle and jumped in after them. Yevgeny reached the main road at the end of the quayside, turned right over the canal bridge and drove fast up the hill out of Bude towards Upton and Widemouth Bay.

Yevgeny didn't stop, he drove down the A39, then took the A395 across to the A30 which he stayed on all the way into central Exeter where they dumped their BMW having taken all their bags out and wiped it clean of their prints. Before walking away Yevgeny used a short stout metal rod to prise off the number plates which both broke; the pieces were dropped into a bin as they walked. It wasn't perfect but it would buy time and confuse any investigators.

They then took a cab to Exeter Airport where they rented a

new car, using new identity documents they had been carrying with them all the time. Three hours later they were back in Bude and using new identities were checking into the Premier Inn Hotel. Alexei's almost bald head was now covered with a wig and Yevgeny wore glasses and a moustache. They still had a job to do and intended to do it.

The entire group came together and surrounded Igor and Magd outside the front of the Falcon. Igor looked at Gerald and Maddie who were standing watching him half lying, half sitting on the ground. The light of recognition went on in his eyes as he recognised the couple.

Gerald knelt beside him and said, "Hello Igor, it has been a while. Stay here, there is an ambulance on its way."

Igor grinned weakly and nodded, "Not a good day for the sharks, my friend, eh?"

"I guess not," agreed Gerald.

Ros had commandeered the Bude police station to be used as a temporary holding area for those now under arrest. SBS Sergeant Jim Sweeney and his men were already there guarding their earlier prisoners, and now the whole group, a police van and an ambulance made its way to the little police station which was about to become very busy and crowded. The turning to the Bude police station is up a little slope in the centre of town and two policemen stood in the road at the bottom of the slope to prevent access by the public.

Igor was quickly assessed and the doctor dealt with his relatively minor gunshot flesh wound. Alexei's bullet had passed clean through his upper thigh without causing any internal damage. Igor, Daoud and Akram were all walking wounded and it had been decided earlier that casualties without life-threatening injuiries would not go to hospital. Instead they would stay with the group, closely guarded and out of the public eye. A Royal Naval surgeon, a doctor and a nurse had been flown by helicopter from Plymouth to provide the medical help the three men needed.

Later that night, just before the light started going, the prisoners were taken from the police station and, with blankets over their heads, were loaded into a police prison van to be driven to GCHQ at Morwenstow.

The press and public were by now all over Bude in large numbers, and TV cameras set up at the bottom of the slope, as well as press photographers, all recorded the prisoners being loaded onto the van. The small convoy, consisting of the prison van, its guard vehicles and five other vehicles, were escorted by police motorcycle riders through three road blocks along the route which prevented the press or public from following them to GCHQ.

Gerald, Maddie and Ros were all in Gerald's Range Rover which was part of the convoy.

From the back seat Ros commented, "Well, folks, that was part one. We've got them all and we have the proof of what they intended. Now it's interrogation and confession time, and Gerald, you have got to cuddle up to your old pal Igor and get him to really open up."

They drove on in silencre, then she spoke again. "By the way, we sent a navy helicopter after the *Annie Mae* but she must have been underway for a while, because she just made international waters before we could stop her."

26

The satellite dishes and buildings of GCHQ Morwenstow lie within a secure, patrolled perimeter fence, and the whole area is monitored in several ways which are closely guarded secrets.

When planning started for the operation Ros and her colleagues at MI6 had decided that, if the operation succeeded, the aftermath procedures of interrogations, debriefings and, if necessary, medical care would all be conducted within the secure envelope of the GCHQ site, away from the media and any other prying eyes.

Work had been ongoing for the past week, preparing two adjacent buildings where prisoners could be held securely, they and their security guards could sleep, and all those involved could work, eat and be accommodated as necessary.

Captain Kerr and his men remained on loan from the Royal Navy to guard the prisoners and provide an extra inner ring of security.

Gerald was sitting in a small lounge at a coffee table flicking through a selection of the daily newspapers. In varying degrees of accuracy the Bude incident was reported in all of them.

They all carried a statement released by the Home Office which spoke of a terrorist attack on the GCHQ complex having been foiled by the security services. The statement continued that the terrorists were all in custody in a secure government location, and there had been no casualties except one armed terrorist who had been killed resisting arrest. It concluded by promising there would be a more comprehensive statement in the next few days.

There was a knock on the door and Corporal Tod Pollard stood aside to let Igor enter. Igor was wearing handcuffs.

"Good morning, Boss, just delivering your guest." Pollard made the introduction, which he didn't realise was unnecessary, then he stepped back and stood at attention inside the closed door.

Igor Petrov, looking pale and tired, smiled weakly at Gerald who stood to greet him, holding out his hand. Igor raised both hands which prompted Gerald to turn to the corporal.

"Tod, please get the key, there is no need for these cuffs. Mr Petrov and I are old friends."

The key was in his pocket and looking wary, Tod Pollard took the handcuffs off Igor before resuming his guard position inside the door.

Gerald gestured to Igor to sit opposite him and to the corporal he said, "Thanks, Tod, I'll take it from here and call you when I need you."

"I will be right outside, Sir," said the SBS man as he stepped out of the room and closed the door.

"It has been a long time, Igor, how about some coffee?"

Igor's Moscow controllers had ordered his execution, so it was obvious there was no possibility of turning him and sending him back to Moscow as a double agent working for MI6. This made Gerald's job much easier. There was now only one option and one set of objectives.

Ros and two men from MI6, who had arrived the night

before, had briefed Gerald that what they wanted was a full confession and a complete mental download of everything Igor knew that might be of interest to Western intelligence. If he cooperated Igor would go free, would be given a new identity and could live anywhere he liked in the West where he would be able to be kept safe.

"I am sorry you got shot, Igor, and I am sorry your man was killed."

The Russian shrugged and replied, "I am OK, a flesh wound, and the painkillers work. He wasn't my man, a Syrian mercenary doing a job, he knew the risks."

Gerald and Igor talked through the morning and had sandwiches and coffee sent in at lunchtime. Standing guard outside the door Corporal Pollard could only hear the hum of voices, occasional laughter and sometimes a door opening and closing when Gerald or Igor used the adjoining toilet.

There were microphones in the room, and close by, down the corridor, Ros and her MI6 colleagues were listening to, and recording, every word. The listeners soon realised that the decision to involve Gerald had really paid off. Not only had Gerald and his people been highly effective in the field, but his involvement in the interview and debriefing stage was also working as well as they could ever have hoped.

Igor was no fool, and he quickly realised that it was his own side which had tried to kill him. This didn't just make Gerald's job easier, it was a total game changer.

It was obvious even to the listeners who couldn't see what was happening that there was a chemistry between the two men. Gerald was in no hurry and the conversation started with enquiries about each other's families, health, financial circumstances and other personal issues. The talk then went to shark fishing and old times and, chuckling, Igor told Gerald that he had always suspected Gerald wasn't what he pretended to be.

The pair agreed that the world was in a mess and they both said they thought their respective governments were useless. Cold War days were remembered almost fondly as they agreed it had been a different world back then, and in many ways a safer one. At least it had been a world in which nations had mostly been led by better leaders than those in power today, and people like Gerald and Igor played by a certain set of rules within known parameters.

It wasn't until after lunch, several hours after the interview had started, that Gerald told Igor what he wanted and what the UK could give in return. Igor knew he had no option other than to agree, but he did so with one caveat on which everything depended. He would start talking only when he had proof that MI6 had got his wife and two sons out of Russia and they were in a safe place.

This request had been foreseen and as far as possible had been planned for. Gerald didn't tell Igor this, but he did say that now they would have to be joined by his friends. He emphasised "friends", meaning Ros and her MI6 colleagues.

Igor agreed and Gerald said they would take a break to get some fresh air before they reconvened with the MI6 people. Gerald and Igor strolled together around the GCHQ site, but were always careful not to move into open areas which would be visible to anyone watching from outside the perimeter. Alexei's sniper shot had missed yesterday, but the Russian hit men were still at large, and Igor might not be so lucky a second time.

When they reconvened Ros took the lead. She told Igor, who nodded and smiled, that she had been listening to him talking to Gerald all morning and the conversation had been recorded.

She thanked him for co-operating and agreed to his condition. She confessed that MI6 had foreseen this as a possibility and had a snatch team already in place in Moscow.

Igor didn't need telling that speed was essential if the extraction of his family was to succeed. Ros needed to know as exactly as possible what the family's movements were day by day. Crucially she wanted to identify a time when Igor's wife and his two sons were likely to be together and by themselves. The next day was Sunday and Igor knew that it was almost certain that his family would follow a familiar routine and drive to Igor's sister-in-law for a family lunch.

Ros instantly recognised the opportunity this would present. Igor's wife and their sons would be together in one car and on the move. It would be easy for the snatch team to follow them and check that no one else was doing so. If the family was not under surveillance the snatch team would intercept them and take them to a safe house from where they could talk to Igor. As long as they all wanted to come to the West they would stay at the safe house for a couple of days while documents with new identities were prepared, their appearances altered and then all three would leave Russia separately using different road border crossing points.

If they didn't want to join Igor they would be released and the Chechen mercenaries who MI6 often used for such tasks, would just disappear. If either one of his two sons did not want to come to the West he would be held until the others were safely out of Russia and would then be released. The plan was simple; there was no reason to believe it wouldn't succeed.

Ros pushed Igor hard for his view as to whether both his sons would want to leave their lives and their country. Igor was confident the whole family would want to leave for a new life in the West, but said that obviously his conversation with his family would confirm this. Ros left the room to communicate with the Chechens and give them the green light for the snatch and the extraction which, hopefully, would follow.

Igor, Gerald, Ros and the MI6 group at GCHQ would now spend twenty-four hours waiting for the snatch and for Igor to talk to his family.

In the meantime while waiting for the call, Ros and her colleagues started the interrogations with Magd and the five other Syrians. It was unlikely that Suleiman's death would ever be acknowledged or recorded, or that his body would ever leave the UK. However, Ros gave orders that the body be frozen until the whole interrogation and debriefing process had been completed.

Bude's pubs, cafés, restaurants were all awash with excited speculation and rumour. Whenever people met, whether it was families, friends, acquaintances, or even strangers, the conversation would be about the terrorist attack.

On Friday night and all day Saturday Alexei and Yevgeny toured bars and cafés, hoping to find out where the British authorities were now holding their targets. Everyone wanted to talk and there was no lack of theories and counter-theories as to what had happened and what would now happen.

One particularly "brilliant" local wanted to bring back the death penalty and another didn't want Muslims to be punished by death because they would die happily thinking they were on their way to heaven and the seventy-two virgins that awaited them. Instead this second "genius" wanted the Muslims to be punished by spending the rest of their lives in jail being force-fed pork scratchings.

All sorts of in-the-know locals were happy to give Alexei and Yevgeny their version of events, most of them knew nothing other than what had been broadcast on the newsmedia.

But three people who didn't boast about what they knew, clearly had some knowledge. All, separately, told the same story, which was that all the terrorists were being held in the GCHQ complex at Morwenstow.

One man's sister had seen the convoy driving through the gate into the GCHQ site, a woman knew someone who knew someone who worked as a cleaner at GCHQ and had for the past few days been helping prepare two buildings for the arrival of some mystery guests. The third piece of information was from a dog walker from Morwenstow who the previous evening had noted that there were now several armed guards with dogs patrolling the fence inside the perimeter of the complex. He was sure this was a new development.

By mid-afternoon on Saturday the two Russian killers had become enthusiastic hikers. They had visited a sports shop in Bude's Strand, and wearing all the same clothing as worn by hikers and walkers they were now carefully exploring the area around the GCHQ site.

27

Magd was of considerably greater intelligence value than the six men he had recruited. The five Syrian survivors had little of interest to tell Ros's MI6 interrogators. However, Magd was in a different league and knew a lot that was of considerable value about Syria now that the Assad family had left. The country was a complex web of militias, sects and personalities. He understood he was going to spend a very long time in a British prison.

During Saturday afternoon and evening, and Sunday morning he was quizzed continually. He released information slowly as if he thought he could use it as currency to bargain with. He kept saying there was more he could say if he was given assurances of a reduced sentence. No assurances were given but neither were the negotiators absolutely clear that no deals were possible.

By lunchtime on Sunday Ros and her colleagues were confident that Magd had told them all he knew about Igor's operation and present day Syria. However, there was also much that he knew about Russian and Iranian arms dealing, so the questioning continued.

The five Syrians agreed to sign confessions; they would all be charged and, like Magd, they would be sent to a new home in Belmarsh High Security Prison. Their trial would be public because a part of the MI6 plan was to make the trial as embarrassing to Russia as possible.

Although the five men had thought they were working for

an Islamic organisation, Magd had known the truth, and in return for promises of absolute protection from possible Russian assassins, and vague hints that his information might help with an early release, Magd was ready to point a finger confirming that the plan had been hatched and enabled by the FSB and the SVR in Moscow.

As long as Igor's condition could be met and his family got out of Russia, then he would also state publicly in court that the attacks had been planned and ordered by the government of the Russian Federation. As always the Russians would deny everything and construct an alternative narrative and hide behind it, but seven witnesses on public trial and all the evidence that had been gathered would leave the world in no doubt as to where guilt lay.

Moscow is two hours ahead of London and by mid-afternoon on Sunday nerves in GCHQ Morwenstow were jangling as the tension mounted while those involved waited for the Chechen snatch gang to communicate via a secure link and enable Igor to talk to his family. At 5:00 pm UK time, 7:00 pm Russian time, Igor was talking to his wife and sons. For half an hour he talked of the new life of freedom that awaited them in the West if they wanted it. Igor had worried that there might be reluctance or resistance from his elder son but there wasn't.

Igor ended the conversation with his family by saying they would all be together in a few days. Ros then spent time talking to her Chechen group who were essentially gangsters, smugglers and guns for hire. There was always the concern whether such people could be trusted. But this group were as good as it gets, they had interests in the West, family members in the West and hated the Russian government.

Ros agreed that on Wednesday all three of Igor's family members would be separately driven to border crossings in Poland and the Baltic States en route to being reunited in Berlin and then flown to London.

Ros went through the arrangements with Igor in as much detail as she had. No chances would be taken with civilian travel arrangements. From Berlin Igor's family would be flown to the UK by the Royal Air Force. Once Igor and his family were re-united he would start to talk freely and without any reservations until MI6 knew everything that he knew.

During Igor's debriefing period the family's new Canadian identities and life histories would be worked on, and then after the public trial it would be declared that Igor Petrov would spend the rest of his life in mostly solitary confinement in Belmarsh High Security Prison. In fact, he and his family would disappear.

During Saturday Alexei and Yevgeny patrolled the area around GCHQ. Using binoculars and getting as close as they could in several places without attracting attention, they were able to substantiate that there were guards with dogs on patrol and there were a number of buildings in which Igor and Magd could be held while being interrogated.

Several ordinary vehicles were seen coming and going but no helicopters had taken off or landed. The assassins decided there had to be a good chance that their information had been correct and their targets were still in GCHQ.

They believed the best, and possibly the only, chance they would have of killing Igor and Magd would be to lie and wait in ambush hoping they left the camp in vehicles rather than by helicopter. In case they were moved by helicopter Alexei had identified a good lying-up position and this was from where they watched the camp with Alexei's rifle and an RPG in readiness. It was more likely that vehicles would be used and if this happened they would leave the main GCHQ gate and turn left. They would then drive straight for about half a mile to a crossroads where they would turn right heading for Woodford Cross and Shop. Once through the village of Shop it was then less than two miles to the main A39 road. After leaving Shop there is a small garden business called Pete's Plants on the right. About half-way between Pete's Plants and the A39 is a large pull-in to a gateway which opens onto a field where there are wind turbines.

The Russians had already chosen the gateway as their waiting position for a road ambush. They would be able to see vehicles approaching, destroy them and then be on the A39 making their escape in less than half a mile.

As it was getting dark on Sunday evening Alexei was watching the camp and saw men being led out and loaded into a police van. He raced to his vehicle and jumped in shouting at Yevgeny to drive fast to the roadside ambush position they had already selected.

The police waited until it was fully dark and then a prison van followed by an unmarked police car took exactly the route that the Russian killers had anticipated and where, unknown to them, Alexei and Yevgeny now waited in ambush.

Richard and Ox had not known that the police were moving the Syrians after dark on Sunday. They had no real reason to be at GCHQ because their part of the operation had now ended. However, they had nothing to do in Bude, and the whole gang were at GCHQ; so they spent the afternoon there chatting, drinking and playing snooker with Maddie, Andy, Jackie, Christine, George and the others.

Everyone had left by 9:00 pm except Maddie, who was waiting for Gerald, who was still working with Igor, Ros and the MI6 people.

Richard and Ox stayed to keep Maddie company, and eventually left GCHQ about ten minutes before the prison van drove out of the gate with its prisoners on board. They took the obvious route back to the A39 which was the route that the prison van would also follow in a few minutes.

They drove by Pete's Plants heading for the main road. Their conversation stopped when they passed Alexei and Yevgeny parked and waiting in their ambush position. A number of factors combined to prevent Alexei and Yevgeny realising they had seen Richard and Ox before. They were in Jackie's Land Rover which the Russians hadn't already seen, the light had almost gone and there was no light inside the Land Rover. Ox's face was half obscured by a beanie which was pulled down over his ears, and his head was turned towards Richard who was driving.

"Did you see who that was?" Richard asked Ox.

"Sure did, I wonder what the hell they are doing waiting there?"

"Don't know, but whatever they are planning you can be sure it will be something naughty. I am sure they didn't see us, let's check them out."

Just before reaching the A39 there was a pull-in on the left with a gate into a field with wind turbines.

"Let's leave the Landy here, run back through the field, come up behind the two lover boys and wish them Happy Christmas, or something like that."

"You got it," said Ox who was already getting out of the vehicle.

They quickly ran the nearly half mile inside the hedge in the dark field back to where the Russians were parked. They stood behind the hedge about forty yards from the Russians panting heavily.

"Wow, I'm unfit," said Ox gasping for air.

"Unfit," said Richard, "We're not unfit, pal, we are just getting older."

"Speak for yourself, buddy. Now what?" asked Ox.

"We'll wait another short while to get our breath back; then one of us will creep up on each side of their car. Then simultaneously when we get to them we will wish them Happy Christmas." Richard stopped whispering, waited 20 seconds and then nodded to Ox. They crept along the hedge and came up behind the Russians' car glad to be approaching with the help of the darkness.

While Alexei and Yevgeny waited they ate the sandwiches they had brought with them. Apart from the sandwiches, they had crisps, drinks and fruit in the car because they had known the stakeout of the GCHQ camp was likely to last for a long period. Next to the food and drinks on the other half of the back seat were two Kalashnikov automatic rifles and an RPG.

Once they had destroyed the vehicles and killed the occupants they planned to dump their weapons and drive straight to London Heathrow. They couldn't foresee how many vehicles they would have to deal with. Their plan was to stop the lead prison vehicle with the RPG (rocket propelled grenade), and then, if there were any survivors, they would use their automatic weapons to kill them, together with the occupants of any other vehicles.

It was a warm early summer evening and their front car

windows were half open on both sides for fresh air and so that they could hear when vehicles approached.

Even though it was dark Richard and Ox knew that their approach for the last few yards would be very dangerous. They couldn't know exactly how visible they might be in the mirrors of the Russian's vehicle; so first they stooped, then crawled, and then slithered forward on their bellies. They still had their pistols which they held in front of them.

They reached the back of the car unseen and lay there for a few seconds to see if their approach had been noticed and would provoke a reaction. There was half a red brick beside Richard and using sign language he signalled to Ox that he would chuck the brick to his right, to create a small diversion which would allow them to stand up, and hopefully get the Russians out of their vehicle.

The half brick crashed into the hedge, the front doors of the Russians' vehicle flew open and Alexei and Yevgeny leapt out to investigate the noise. Both were holding Kalashnikov rifles.

"Happy Christmas," said Richard not wishing to miss the opportunity to crack his little joke. The end of the barrel of his pistol was inches from Yevgeny's head. "Drop the gun."

Yevgeny hesitated and looked at Alexei who nodded. Yevgeny bent to put his weapon on the ground watched by Richard and Ox each of whom had their gun on a Russian. Alexei put his rifle on the ground, then seeing a chance, he reached under his jacket and suddenly was holding a pistol. As he rose and pointed his weapon at Richard there was the sharp sound of a shot fired at close range.

For a split second Richard wondered whether Alexei had shot and missed, then he saw him jerk violently backwards and crumple to the ground in a heap.

"Happy Christmas," said Ox with his gun still pointing at the now prone figure of Alexei. "I had no choice, Richard, he was pulling the trigger to shoot you."

"I owe you," replied Richard in a sombre voice, as he moved to push Yevgeny back away from his weapon which he picked up. He had no handcuffs, rope or cable ties so used his belt to secure Yevgeny's hands behind his back. While he was tying him up the large prison police vehicle, followed by the unmarked police car passed by, heading for the main road. Neither the prisoners nor their police escort realised they had just sailed past what might have been a deadly ambush.

Richard called Ros at GCHQ and she sent the SBS captain and one of his men to retrieve Alexei's body and bring Yevgeny back to GCHQ. Like the others Yevgeny co-operated with his interrogators in the hope of spending reduced time in prison. He not only had a lot to say regarding his orders to kill Igor and Magd, but he also confessed to having carried out other killings in Western countries which had never been solved by the police forces concerned.

Gerald and Maddie had been about to go home to Bude when Richard's call came through to Ros. They accompanied the SBS men to where Richard and Ox stood waiting for them with one live Russian and one dead one.

After the SBS men had left, taking their prisoner and the body back with them to GCHQ, Gerald gave Richard and Ox a lift up the road to where they had left the Land Rover. As they were getting into the vehicle Gerald said, "We'll go home to Bude, get a bottle of wine and meet you on the tables in front of the café on Crooklets Beach."

The night was warm and still, it was almost an African night. The light of the moon bathed the land and the sea in a silver glow. The four people sitting at a table were clearly visible sitting next to their moonshadows. The tide was right out and the whole sandy beach stretched out in front of them. Under the beach lay the still intact cable so vital to the UK's communications. No one said anything as they sipped their wine and thought of what might have been.

After a while Gerald raised his glass and said, "Here's to explosions that didn't happen, and staying ahead of the game."

The only sounds were those of the sea and four wine glasses being clinked together.

28

The next day Igor, Gerald and Ros flew by helicopter to a small village nestled in the Chiltern Hills where there was a high security fully guarded MI6 safe house which would be Igor's new home until he and his family disappeared after the public trial.

Maddie and the whole original team had gone to Tiverton Castle to pack up and wait until the end of the week when Gerald and Ros had said something special would happen.

On Friday came the news that Gerald and Ros had been waiting for. An RAF plane had taken off from Berlin heading for Northolt Airfield in Ruislip, North London. From the airfield Igor's wife and two sons would be driven at high speed to a family reunion.

Igor had scores to settle, his own country had tried to kill him, his debriefing took nearly three weeks and he held nothing back.

As soon as Igor's family was safe in the Chiltern Hills the British government released a detailed statement accusing The Russian Federation of planning and trying to carry out an attack against a NATO country. In an echo from Igor's past Britain expelled seven Russian diplomats and various other NATO countries also expelled Russian diplomats to support Britain and underline the point being made.

Moscow denied all the allegations and blamed the attack on

terrorists which it was hinted, might have been NATO plants carrying out a false flag attack to embarrass Russia. No one believed the Russian denials, and a month later when the trials began and the witnesses gave their statements the Kremlin didn't even bother with further denials, there was no point.

Ros's Kremlin source reported that Putin had gone beserk as the true scale and the level of embarrassment became evident. Several FSB and SVR officers lost their jobs and ended their lives living in disgrace, and there were rumours of executions carried out to set an example and send a chilling message to those working in Russian intelligence that failure would not be tolerated.

Ros decided she had earned the right to flaunt her position a little and commandeered an RAF helicopter to fly her and Gerald back to Tiverton late on Friday afternoon. At eight o'clock that night Gerald's original gang, Maddie, Ros, Richard, Ox, Andy, Jackie, Christine, George, Henry and William were all in the dining room, drinking to the success of their mission.

Tom and Fiona Edworthy had disappeared in the middle of the afternoon and hadn't been seen since. Now, with Tom at her shoulder, Fiona Edworthy walked into the room and clapped her hands. "Chop-chop children, outside on the lawn, please. There is an 'old deer' waiting to say hello."

Tables and chairs had been set up in a semi-circle around a large spit on which a whole red deer carcass was slowly turning as it roasted.

George's mouth dropped open and he said, "Spiffing, just what the doctor ordered." Then he went quiet as he counted the number of chairs and tables. Including the Edworthy's there should have been thirteen; there were twenty. George was just about to say something, when a gravelly voice behind him said, "Hands in the air, everyone!" and six SBS men stepped out of their hiding places grinning grins that split their faces.

"Are we invited?" asked Captain Jonathan Kerr.

"No," said another voice and Cole Benson came into view holding his shotgun.

"Put that bloody thing away," was shouted in unison by everyone present.

"OK, but where is my beer then?" asked Cole.

By 11:00 pm a huge amount of acohol had been drunk and the red deer was a skeleton. Before everyone started drifting off Gerald called for attention and proposed a toast.

"Here's to being ahead of the game and staying there."

Twenty glasses were raised and twenty mouths made various noises of assent. Richard was standing next to Ros, he took her hand and gave it a stroke and a squeeze.

"Later," she whispered, which Maddie overheard and which prompted an exaggerated wink from her in Richard's direction. *Bugger*, thought Richard, *that woman doesn't miss a thing*.

EPILOGUE

In the days following June Symonds's rape by Magd her cuts and bruises had healed. The mental damage was taking longer to repair itself; the violent images of the events of that night often re-surfaced and woke her in the darkness.

She and her brother Reuben were sitting at home at their kitchen table having cups of tea and half watching the BBC South West evening news. They suddenly paid more attention as they saw a line of men with blankets over their heads being loaded into a large police van.

"… *the police made an announcement at lunchtime today regarding the arrest in Bude of several men believed to be foreign nationals. It is understood that senior officials from the Home Office are in Bude and a government statement will be issued in the morning. Speculation is rife that a major terrorism incident has been averted. Locals witnessed activity close to shore involving several small vessels, then the boats went into Bude harbour where a number of armed men brought ashore what looked like several prisoners who were taken away in unmarked vans to Bude police station.*

"*One man was clearly injured because he had to have help when coming ashore, and he, together with two men on stretchers, left in an ambulance. The men were later moved under armed escort to an undisclosed destination.*

"*Hugh and Clare Macleod from Stratton near Bude were on the cliffs above the seapool and watched the drama unfold:*

"'*We heard what sounded like gunshots out at sea off Crooklets which came from two boats close together. At that distance we couldn't*

253

see clearly what was happening, but there were several shots and it looked like some sort of gun battle. Then about ten minutes later two other small boats came from the Northcott direction and joined them, they all came into the harbour where everyone got off all four boats. Some men were in handcuffs and were obviously prisoners because the others were supervising them at gunpoint. We also saw two stretchers being loaded into an ambulance.'"

As Hugh Macleod finished talking to the TV interviewer the last of the prisoners was stepping up into the police vehicle, and as he did so, the blanket slipped off his head and Magd turned and looked full into the camera.

June's heart stopped, she gasped, uttered a little cry of surprise, her hand flew to her mouth and tears rolled down her cheeks.

Reuben looked from the television to his sister and then back again. "That bastard."

Almost in a whisper June said, "He is going to prison, I hope he never gets out. Now I think I will be able to sleep again at night."

SHARK CORNWALL PUBLISHING

Shark Cornwall Publishing